Fetish
Sterling and Anita

By
Nadine Frye

I

Acknowledgments

First, I want to thank Allah for giving me a gift to share with the world. Islam saved my life, and I pray that His light was always upon my soul.

Next, my husband, Anwar Scott, there is nothing in the world like your love. Thank you for loving a woman who came in pieces, and you glued her back together. I would not trade anything in the world for the nights we share our dreams. The way you randomly start chopping, the laughter we share, praying with you, fasting with you, watching you raise the boys to be men, and your ability to motivate me into my better self. I will continue to write these books while you spread awareness through your platform @DMVHOODZNDNEWZ. I am proud of who you are becoming as a man.

I have the best family in the world. To every Frye, Taylor, Jones, Buxton, Young, Hampton, and Royal that encouraged me and pushed me, I love you all, and this journey was for you as well as me.

My children are my everything, and two of the greatest gifts Allah could have bestowed upon me. Aaqil and Isa are the funniest, loving, smart, caring, and protective sons in the world. Can't wait to watch them grow into Kings and leading their own families. I want a bunch of grandchildren that I can spoil and send back to your house tipping. It may be many years before I get my dream, but in shaa Allah, I will see it.

To Monica, Tiff, and Desaree, you guys are more than Authors that I've bonded with. You've held me up when I faltered, laughed with me, cried with me, prayed for me, and just motivated me to keep fighting in this industry. I love you all, and I promise this sisterhood shall not be broken, and we are rocking for life.

To every last one of my readers/fans, thank you for allowing me to have a platform that you enjoy. Thank you for letting my creativity keep my books in your hands. There are no limits to my mind, so I hope you are here for its many facets.

To Mesha,

Thank you for always being a friend to me and supporting me when I was a newbie in the game. I appreciate all of the late-night conversations about life and how to navigate this book world. Now you have allowed me to join a fantastic team, and it's only one way to go from here, and that's up.

To My MMP Sisters,

Understand that this year, our possibilities are endless. We are coming to change the game, and I need every one of you to put game faces on, and let's run these lanes over. Stay committed, ladies.

Prologue

It was a dreary Saturday morning, and my house was alive with activity. I could hear my mother downstairs cleaning to the old school sounds of Maze featuring Frankie Beverley. My mother's voice carried through our home full of happiness and determination. Beyond the right wall in my room, Saturday morning cartoons played on a mid-volume from my sister's room. They were just a bedroom over, and you could hear the merriment that only a weekend could give children.

Everyone seemed alive and happy, and that was a regular Saturday routine at my house. I, on the other hand, sat in my bedroom, in my closet, with a notebook and pen. Writing stories was my absolute favorite past time and brought me immense joy. I was trying my best to get lost inside of a story that would allow me to live outside of my reality. Even if only for a little while. I heard someone enter my room, and it made me jump a little. I chuckled at my overreaction when I remembered it was daytime. Knowing that it wasn't night time made me feel safe. But not secure enough to reveal my whereabouts.

"Sterly, where are you? Mama wants you to come downstairs and clean the ceiling fans because none of us can reach it in the chair."

It was just my sister Shelisa, so I breathed a little more smoothly and came out of the closet.

"Okay, tell her I am coming right now," I said, barely above a whisper.

I hated talking to anyone. I hit puberty, but my voice hadn't caught the deepness that was indicative of the coming of young adulthood.

"Boy, what's wrong with you? Speak up, I can barely hear you. Sterly, bring your butt downstairs before mama comes up here to get you. You know you don't want that."

I hurriedly put my notebook up in its hiding place, cut off the lamp that I had placed in there, and get to moving. One thing you don't do is keep Sherlise Carter waiting for anything. My mom was a single mom from the streets of North Philly, and she had no problem reminding us of that point. She'd be the first to tell you of all that she did to ensure that we didn't want for anything.

On Saturdays, she would get to preaching. Please don't think you would lay in bad past seven comfortably. If

you did, Sherlise Carter would scream from the rooftops
that it wasn't comfortable raising three children by herself
and how the least we could do after she worked hundred-
hour weeks was to keep her house clean. So, when she said
move, you put your body in motion before she applied foot
to ass.

I rushed down the stairs and headed into the
kitchen. My mother was focused on her task of scrubbing
the stove as she sang her heart out. When I got to the
entranceway, I stood and watched her, not wanting to
interrupt her flow. I was watching her for a while when she
finally looked up and became startled.

"Shit, son, you scared me half to death. Announce
yourself when entering a room. You know my nerves are
bad."

"Yes, ma'am," I humbly responded

"Speak up, Boy Child. I can hardly hear you.
What's wrong with you? You have been acting very weird
lately. All timid, skittish, and whatnot. Are you on drugs? I
hope not because I have worked too hard to keep my young
from being crackheads."

I smiled at my mother's crazy talk.

"No, ma'am," I said a little bit louder than before to be sure she heard me.

"Good, now grab the duster, get on up in the chair, and clean those ceiling fan blades. I don't know whose bright idea it was to create ceiling fans, but I'm almost certain that they were biased against the height-challenged. Ooooh, that's my jam."

And just like that, I had a chore, and the subject was changed. I set about the task of cleaning the ceiling fans throughout the downstairs. I started in the dining room and then proceeded to the living room. To make the job as painless as possible, I made sure to grab a dust cloth and wipe off the surfaces underneath the fans. If I knew my mama, I knew that she would be checking for that very thing. I was wiping down the sofas when I heard my mother call my name.

"Ma'am?!"

"Come here, child. I need you to do me a favor."

I finished the last of the dusting and headed into the kitchen to see what she needed.

"You called me, mama?"

"Yes, boy, I need you to take these clothes downstairs to the basement and run them through the *washer. Your sisters are so forgetful when it comes to their chores. They are just good for nothing."*

I visibly flinched because I did not want to go into the basement. Bad things happened in the basement. If my mom only knew, I'm sure she would not send me down there.

"Boychild, I swear you are making me question life. What the hell is wrong with you now? You look like you are afraid of your own shadow. I see I'm going to need your uncle to toughen you up some more. You're acting abnormal, and I ain't raising no punk bitches. All the training you do with your uncle, it seems like you should be just a little manlier. Now grab that basket and get to moving them feet before I feel inclined to inspire you."

Inside I was crying. I wouldn't drop tears on the outside because that would just anger her. My mama said boys are not supposed to cry. We are supposed to face our obstacles and move on. My mother's greatest fear was that I would be soft and swallowed up by the streets.

With resignation, I grabbed the basket and got prepared to go in the basement. Each step that I took triggered my defense mechanisms. In my mind, I was on a mission in a faraway land—a land where I was the ruler, and I stood mighty and powerful. I quietly maneuvered my way down the stairs and then into the laundry room. Quickly, I started putting the clothes in the washer. After, I added the liquid detergent and closed the lid. As I reached over to set the machine, I began to breathe easy because I was almost free from the basement. Now all I have to do was make it back upstairs to finally taste freedom.

I stepped back, preparing to turn around and ran into something hard. Instantly, I became paralyzed with fear. I already knew the only thing behind me was the thing that composed my many nightmares. My limbs trembled as I felt its breath on my neck. I needed to disappear fast. Please, God, just let me teleport to a different place. My nightmare pressed closer to my back, and then a hand closed around my midsection. Then, it whispers in my ear, and my soul began leaving my body.

"You were just going to bring your sexy little ass down here and just not speak to me? Don't you think that was a little rude, my little bottom boy?"

I automatically started crying because its touch was anything but loving. No, their touch was only meant to subdue, overpower, and bend to its will. When the nightmare notices my tears, he licked them from the side of *my face where my birthmark lied. His saliva felt like molten lava, and it was causing my panic to rise.*

"I don't know why you cry so much. You should be proud to be my special little bottom boy. Bitch, you know your tears make my dick hard as a rock."

He proved that statement when he grinded against me while reaching around and stroking my manhood.

This feeling of helplessness and disgust was about to make me lose my lunch. The nightmare began to run his hands all over my adolescent body.

Disappear just disappear, was all I could think while trying to will myself away from the situation.

"It's been so long since I played with my sweet little bottom bitch. Feels like forever since I felt your cheeks wrapped around me. I am getting so aroused just thinking of it. You should get on your knees and warm me up, and then I can slide right inside of you."

I began to struggle against the nightmare. Then, the nightmare placed its hands around my throat and squeezed forcefully.

"We have been going through this too long for you not to realize it only gets worse when you struggle. Now get on your knees and assume the position before I fuck you up,

and we know I hate to waste time when we have so little. Now get down there and swallow my dick like a good little bitch."

Nightmare let my neck go before they stepped back and dropped their pants. I already knew the routine. Just as I was about to assume the position, my mother started screaming for me, and she sounded pissed.

"Sterling, get up here now, and I mean right now!"

Nightmare snatched up their pants at the sound of my mother's voice. Just like always, they only wanted to move around the shadows in the dark and hide their true nature. I got off the floor and immediately felt relieved. I was saved by the bell once again, and I was grateful for small miracles.

I raced upstairs, and my mother was no longer in the kitchen. I went in search of my mother. When I got out of the kitchen, I could see through the front of my house. At a glance, I could see my mother pacing back and forth. I didn't know what had her so worked up. But when she was like this, there was no reasoning with her. She turned to me with tears in her eyes, and that made me nervous.

"Son, don't just stand there. I need you to come in here and make me understand what these folks are telling

me. They are not making sense, and I'm about to lose my mind if I don't get answers quickly."

I made my way into the living room, and I saw my school counselor, Ms. Sunday, on the couch. Two police officers were standing in the doorway. My palms began to sweat, and I visibly started to shake. Ms. Sunday looked into my eyes, and it appeared she was trying to lend me some strength. She didn't look at me in the manner that adults did when they showed pity. No, she gazed at me in a way that conveyed that, from this point on, I would be protected from harm.

"Hey, Sterling, how are you doing today?" Ms. Sunday asked me in a soothing voice that made a person feel comfortable enough to open up.

"He is fine. You don't need to talk to him. All I want you to do is say those things you just said to me, in front of him, so that we can clear up this issue, and you all can go about your day."

I already knew why they were there, but I was hoping I could avoid this part. My cry for help had been answered, but I knew it would cause my mother pain. All I knew was that I needed help, and I didn't want to live in fear of Nightmare anymore.

"Well, okay, Ms. Carter, as I stated before. Sterling came to talk to me in confidence about some disconcerting things concerning members of your household. Those things he shared alarmed me, and I felt it was my duty, as a figure in authority, to come assess the allegations," Ms. Sunday said in clarification to all who were present.

"No, what you said to me was that my son told you that my baby brother was fucking on him. Which I know is a motherfucking lie because my favorite brother would never do anything like that. You people are always making small tales into grand stories. Now Sterling, you better tell them, boy child, that they are mistaken so they can get the fuck out of my house."

I cringed at the vulgarity but got saddened at the apathy in which my mother made her statement. Even more than that, it hurt to the middle of my soul because she didn't even believe me. All eyes were on me, and the pressure of their gazes made me want to shrink. Everyone was waiting for my confirmation or for me to make a rebuttal. I wished the floor would come to swallow me up at that moment so I wouldn't have to become the villain. I didn't want to say anything, but since they were here to advocate for me, then I could openly tell my truth.

"It's true, mama. Uncle Gerald has been doing things to me, mama. Bad things. He even makes me do bad things to him. I don't know how else to make him stop."

"You ain't nothing but a liar, and the truth ain't in you. I raised my brother right alongside you and your sisters. Why would you make up these disgusting things? Now I don't know what type of freaky fantasies you have had or been imagining, but you won't put that ugly on my brother."

My mother's words served to break my heart totally. Still, I had to keep trying to make her understand that the person she held in such high esteem, was preying on the son she bore from her very own womb.

"Mama, why won't you believe me? I would never tell you anything but the truth. When you are at work seven days a week, I am stuck here, in this house, trying to keep Uncle Gerald away from me. When he tells you that we are working out, he is making me do disgusting things with him, and If I refuse to do them, he beats me up. You think I am lying around recovering from harsh workouts when it's because I'm fighting to save my manhood. That's the truth, mama, I swear it. You have to believe what I'm telling you."

I tried reaching out for her so that she could offer me a mother's love, but my mother pushed me away. I'd felt dejected and rejected by that one action, and it made me cry.

"My brother is not a faggot, you little piece of shit. I have no questions about his manhood, unlike your little soft as cotton balls ass. My brother is good to you and takes the time out to raise you when your father would not. I don't know if its misplaced affections because he spends extra time with you. But if you fancy yourself in love or whatever it is that happens with your soft bitch ass feelings, then that's your problem. All I know is that you have decided to tell these elaborate tales because my brother does not feel the same, and that's sad. Just know that you will not get away with disrespecting my family name."

My mother said a mouthful, and it destroyed all that I was or ever hoped to be.

"Ms. Carter, you don't have to speak to him in that manner. We're having a very serious conversation, and you are not creating a safe space for him to express his feelings. Do you know how much courage, bravery, and tenacity it took for Sterling to finally open up? Only to have you villainize his efforts. If you are just going to choose

18

sides and discredit, as well as belittle what he has gone through, then I pity your motherhood. It had to be hard to share this not only with his mother but in front of strangers."

Ms. Sunday tried to defend me against my mother's hostility.

"You don't get to tell me what to do concerning my child. I carried his ungrateful ass for ten months and almost died birthing him. Then, I raised the motherfucker for fourteen years with no help or guidance. What he has done, by telling these lies, is a direct affront to my good family name."

"Ms. Carter, with all due respect, your family name bares no importance when a child has been raped and molested. You have a duty as a mother to ensure that he is protected and safe from harm: physical, mental, or emotional. It is your job as his authoritative figure to make sure to close the door on any breaches there are to your child's safety. 'Mother' is not just a title. It is an action, and your actions are deplorable. How can you sit here and watch your child crying out for help and feel nothing?"

Ms. Sunday was almost in tears from the absurdity of my mother's behavior

"Excuse me, bitch! I will not allow you or anyone else the opportunity to sit here and judge me. Nor will you try to make me feel like I have no right to defend my brother against the lies that my son has told. Then, he took it too far, telling those very lies in front of strangers. We are not in the business of exposing family secrets. This matter should have been dealt with within the family.

It is not right to have outsiders chiming in on a situation that has no direct effect on them. Now he has made this family and me into something we are not. That is the only tragedy here. I do not need a child who dares not only to tell a lie but gets strangers involved in his delusions of grandeur. As far as I am concerned, you can take him and his lies and place him in a better home since this home is such a threat to his safety.

I will allow him to pack a bag, and then you can remove him and put him wherever you see fit because he is no longer welcomed here. I will sign over my rights and allow you all to do what I couldn't. Sterling is unworthy of the Carter name, and just know that if you all decide to try and press charges against my brother, I will be standing with him to fight against everything you are trying to do to destroy us."

That was the last day I ever spoke to my mother or saw my sisters. True to her word, she allowed me to pack a bag, and I was even allowed to tell my sister's goodbye. I made sure to grab all of my notebooks and only a few outfits and pictures. They would be the only things I kept of my old life as I headed into unfamiliar territory.

When the counselor removed me from my home and placed me in the foster care system, I just knew my mama would have a change of heart. Each night when I slept, I imagined my mother coming to me and telling me she made a mistake and that she finally believed me. I prayed diligently for God to help change her heart. What I was not ready for were the lengths she went through to let me know she was serious about disassociating herself from me.

When the counselor started calling my immediate family members to try and place me with them, she was met with opposition. Each phone call she made yielded a no and to never call again. Clearly, the news spread fast. Once word got out that I told on my uncle, who was the golden child of the family, I went from being part of a close-knit family to being all alone in the world.

The state brought charges against my abuser. Every day of the trial, I told of the things that transpired in my mother's house right underneath her nose. I watched my family show up in support of this man who robbed me of my innocence and identity. Every day, my family looked at me with disgust and scorn and even made rude remarks and called me a liar as I sat on the stand. My side of the courtroom was empty except for my school counselor, who also ended up being my foster mother.

There was no support for me, not even when my uncle decided to plead to the charges, but claimed no contest to my rendition of the events that happened. At his sentencing I watched, what used to be my family, beg for leniency and sing his praises while I died on the inside. All in all, he only received three years for the abuse against me, and I would go on to serve life being tormented by the residual effects of a predator.

So alone, I stood after that day. Confused about who I was and what I was to become. Innocence destroyed and my manhood in question. I was left with no real understanding of proper relationships. How could a boy who had never lived, but had been shown only the worst in the world, ever be ready to traverse the vast land?

I vowed that day that I would never be a victim again, and I would live life on my terms. The world was a canvass, and I intended to control what was displayed. Nothing in this life would be up for grabs. Using my words, my mind, and my life, I would dominate! That boy would be a victim no longer.

Before They Met

Chapter 1: Sterling

I was moving around my home on a beautiful, sunny Saturday morning. Music played throughout my domain, and I was enjoying the old school vibes. My melodic voice sang along to Al Green's "How Can You Mend a Broken Heart" and the words to the song always resonated with me deeply. I was vigorously cleaning up my home, and this was one routine from my youth, that for the life of me, I couldn't break. It was the only tradition I kept from when I was young, and before I lost my sense of family.

Although I lived alone, I had a compulsive need for order. I despised dirt, chaos, and disorganization. Germs were real, and so were rodents, and I could live with neither. I finished cleaning my bathroom and was satisfied that the area scented of fresh linen bleach. It sparkled and shined. Before leaving out of the bathroom, I washed my hands and headed down the hall into my office.

My office was the most creative space in the house. I completed some of my best work done here. When I stepped into my space, it was as if a feeling of Zen entered my being. As I stared at the décor, I once again became proud. My office was not typical for a bachelor, but it helped me work out things in my mind, and that was the room's sole purpose. The lighting was low, almost soothing, and I didn't have a desk or regular office furniture. Instead, I had bean bags and throw-pillows in mahogany, black, and burgundy. I grabbed my laptop off the shelf and copped a squat to go through my emails.

Reading emails was a task and a half. As I browsed through them, I saw more than a few emails from my fan-site. It made me smile on the inside to see the numerous women from all over the world, offering me everything from their wombs to their souls. It's funny how the idea of me and the things I could do to their body kept their dreams interesting and their lady parts moist. It was just the way I liked them. Wanting, hoping, and praying for one night with me.

By day, I was a tech wizard that dealt in application development. From my success in that arena, I started a mentorship program. A program that catered to the disadvantaged young males in my old neighborhood who dreamed of making waves into technology. I liked to help the young men I mentored become their higher selves and give them hope of achieving their dreams. But by night, I was a national best-selling author by the name of Wet Dream. My followers called me the King of Erotica. I was a man that loved to weave a tantalizing fantasy.

Women of all ages and ethnicities loved my books. They flocked to my social media sites trying to figure out the man behind all their greatest fantasies. My gimmick was that I was a phantom as an author. None of my sites had any pictures, and, to date, I had never attended any book events. That mystery behind my pen had kept me at the top of the charts, it made me a household name, and the very thing you whispered about amongst your friends.

Since no one knew my identity, it drove the masses into a frenzy. I got propositioned so much I had to laugh at the overtures. If the ladies weren't good for anything else, they kept my ego stroked. My lady fans have offered me their virginities, thousands of dollars to get some head, and offered me the position of house: a husband. Those ladies had no censorship nor any shame when it came to trying to meet Wet Dream.

Even more than that, my mysterious persona kept them coming and buying out the book stores. My sales have had kindle crashing with the multitude of downloads I received on my first-day releases. I decided to update my website with a new erotic piece just to keep myself relevant and a favorite amongst my millions of site subscribers.

Soul Connection

As we partake of this ritual,
A joining together of souls
An intimate way of expression that can only be achieved between you and me.

I take a journey through you that's all too familiar.
It is directly related to our past lives
Our rhythm is in sync, and I'm one with you from mental to spiritual.
Division does not exist at this moment,
Only the uniting of our beings made whole
Whispered affections and incoherent uttering's of lovers
Heart to heart caresses of love personified.
The heat from the indisputable knowledge of one another goes from head to toe,
Your dam opens up at the same moment my tumescence reaches forward,
Now our souls have greeted and merged on the plains of ecstasy.

I hit update at the same time an email comes through. Immediately, my heart began to beat uncontrollably as I saw that it was the email I'd patiently waited to receive. With no time to waste, I hurriedly opened the email and read it.

Dear Mr. Carter,

We would like to inform you that we have found your perfect match according to your specifications.

Attached, you will find her profile and her hard and soft limits. You will need to look over everything, and once you agree, we will have your contract sent to her. Send an email with the phrase "press play," and two weeks from Saturday, you will meet her, and we are confident that you will be pleased.

Thank You,

Your Inner Desires

I closed my laptop and thought about that secret part of my life. Being a Dominant has soothed me in ways that words could not. It has made the dark days of my past no longer exist. To have a woman, pliant, subservient, and willing was such a sweet feeling. I tried to imagine what she would be like, and I became giddy with excitement.

I read over her profile, and my heart starts to beat triple time. On paper, she matched me to a "T," but I had to see her in action to decide. No, I am not the most difficult nor harshest Dom. But I do have a specific affinity and needed a woman whose mind I could push to the limits. I do deal with my women using a firm hand, but only if it is absolutely necessary.

I need my submissive to be able to deal with my non-verbal cues. She should understand that her role was essential but not one that required a lot of physical attention. Her body was not a need. Her mind and willingness are all I desired.

I opened the email and kindly responded with *"press play."* The wheels in my mind began turning, and I was sure I could make this work in both of our favors— time to put some things in motion. In two weeks, I would get a new addition to my life, and I was ready for the games to begin.

Chapter 2: Anita

It's all in a day's work. If my name weren't Anita Fox, I would not have believed this day was real. Being part-owner to a successful business was more than work. I was primarily dealing with all of the issues that came with a novelty shop that specialized in sex toys and accessories.

My best friend Ta'iah and I grew this business from an online shop to an actual store. The Purrrfect Kitty was our baby. With her innovative ideas and my sales prowess, we were a team that could not be beaten.

I came into work today already aggravated as fuck because this old couple that was trying to bring that old thing back, didn't read the instructions. His wife wanted me to tell her why her husband passed out while hanging upside down. To which I responded,

"Because the restraints are for your wrist and not your ankles." The lady almost committed murder trying to be freak-nasty at sixty. She hung up on me.

Was it something I said?

Lawd not today, was my only thought as I was ringing up this last customer.

My skin was crawling because, although I grew up in the south, I was not friendly by nature. If my best friend weren't working on such a big order for one of our many picky clients, I wouldn't have agreed to this insufferable duty. People made my defenses go up, and my need to hide rode my back hard.

Once I finished, I gladly put the closed sign on the door to begin the process of closing the register out and getting our deposit ready to go to the bank. Once that task was completed, I headed to the back to tell Ta'iah that I was leaving for the night.

When I got back there, I saw she had pulled out all the stops. She has utilized our showing room, and I loved how she set had it setup. It looks professional but intimate. She even went and sqwuzed (Yes, I said sqwuzed and not squeezed because if you saw this girls' ass and thighs, you would agree) her booty into some skinny jeans and put on some heels with our company's t-shirt. My best friend was looking like more than a snack and it had me feeling a little lesbian-ish for like twenty seconds before I snapped out of my thoughts.

"Look at you, sugar. Are you sure you are not looking to get into a little trouble?" I had to ask because Ta'iah had me ready to bend her over.

I could only imagine what the club's owner would feel.

"Get your lightweight gay ass away from around here. I was trying to think and get my mind right before my presentation. It has to be perfect. Our reputation is on the line."

I laughed at her ass because she was always calling me "lightweight gay." After all, I liked to slap asses and grab titties. Shit, sue me. I just appreciate a beautiful woman and the way she was created. But don't get me fucked up, I liked to look, but it is not the way I swung.

"Why you so nervous, best friend?"

"This is so nerve-wracking. We have to make a good impression on this club owner. It's not only our company name on the line. We have to present ourselves in the best submissive light since we will be joining the scene at this club," she said to me while bouncing around.

Ta'iah was right. We were more than two business owners. We were submissives in search of life-long Dominant. This new club was the opportunity for us to find what we craved more than anything. We needed a good leader and a man that would take our lifestyle from mere play to a way of life for us.

"You need to calm down because you got this in the bag. Trust your knowledge of the products you create. I love you, boo, and don't forget to call me later."

I hugged my best friend, and I made my way home. I lived not too far away from where we had our shop set up. I followed Delaware Avenue down to Columbus Boulevard and then down to Carpenter street. I pulled into the garage on the side of the house and parked my car.

I exited my vehicle before heading inside my parent's home. When I got inside, there was smooth jazz playing, and when I walked into the living room, I could see my parents loving one another. My mother was giving my father a pedicure while he gazed upon her. He peered at her as if love itself resided on her face. It made me smile because that was exactly what I hoped to have one day.

You see, my parents started their relationship in a Dominant/Submissive dynamic. In a time where it was majorly taboo, they beat the odds. Their love story was something that started as just two individuals who catered to each other's sexual fantasies. Then, it eventually became a way of life that bred into love and marriage and a fantastic family dynamic as a bonus. I knew that my

Dominant would have to come with strong leadership because my daddy was the shit.

Excitedly, I raced over to my parents. I was careful not to disturb their setup because my mom had my daddy's hands soaking. So, I grabbed a stool and sat down to my father's right side. I picked up his hand and used the towel that was laid there to dry them off. I wanted to help give him a manicure. My father doted on me with a smile and an affectionate head rub.

"Dumpling, you didn't have to do that. I appreciate you though sugar."

My father's praise made me look at him lovingly and smile right back.

"You know I will do anything for my favorite daddy in the whole wide world."

Both of my parents started giggling at my silliness. A scene like this was the definition of pure joy for me—my parents and the love they shared. I aspired to one day have that same loving relationship that was taboo to society but standard for myself. They gave me a perfect life full of love and attention. They were just fluent together, and I craved what they had.

"Baby, you got some mail. I put it in your room on your bed," my mom told me, and for some reason, my heart began to beat erratically.

"Okay, well, I'm going to go up and get ready for bed. Goodnight, folks."

We showed each other love before I departed. I rushed up the stairs to the third floor of my childhood home. My father had knocked down the walls separating the two rooms when I came home from college. People thought it was weird to be thirty still living at home with my parents, but that was far from the truth.

My parents knew of my affinity for the BDSM lifestyle, and my dad did not want me to leave until I found the perfect Dom to protect me. I was his only daughter, and the thought of me being out in the world alone wrecked his nerves. So, I felt safe at home with them. It was amazing to have the guidance of my parents still.

I saw where my mother had neatly stacked the envelopes on my bed for my perusal. I didn't even want to look just yet, so I started to undress and prepare to complete my night time ablutions.

The shower felt amazing. My best friend gifted me with the newest seasonal fragrance from Knatural

Kreations Spiced Cookies and Tea, and it felt refreshing on my skin. The robust scent of the blood orange mixed with the frankincense made my nerves come alive. Ta'iah swore by this company, and I could see why.

After washing a few times, I stepped out and headed into my room to gather the things I needed to lay down. I grabbed a black silk teddy and put it over my head. Next, I went in my drawer and grabbed the matching thong and slid them up my thighs to my waist. I wrapped my hair before sitting in the middle of the bed to begin dealing with this mail.

Initially, all I saw were bills, bills, bills until I reached the very last envelope. It was from the newest club that Ta'iah and I applied for membership. I was trembling a little and didn't know if I even wanted to open it. On shaky hands, I opened the letter.

Dear Ms. Fox,

You have been chosen to enter a mutually beneficial relationship between Dominant and Submissive in which you are the latter. Upon agreement to the terms that will be stated below, you will become Slave to the Dominant that has been delegated to you using our complex matchmaking system.

Hygiene/Personal Care

A. *You will only be required to bathe in products provided to you by the Dominant. He has a meticulous system and scent relegates his moods.*

B. *Your clothing will be selected and laid out by your Dominant daily, and you will be required to dress in said chosen selections.*

C. *You will have standing Hair and Spa appointments weekly, in which your Dominant will decide which services are required,*

Time Management

A. *Your work schedule must be approved before you commit.*

B. *You are allowed to visit with friends and family under the pre-approval of your dominant.*

C. *You will be required to travel for a week once a month.*

D. *Your car will be outfitted with a tracking device as will your cellular device.*

Rules/Safety

A. As per your profile, we know your hard limits are bestiality, humiliation, and mutilation.

B. If at any time you wish to stop any activity your safe phrase is: "London Bridges." At which time, all activity will end, and you will be free from any business in which you were previously involved.

C. You must be sure to communicate with your Dominant your every move and daily activities so that he may always be able to keep you safe.

D. Your Dominant will use a mixture of verbal and non-verbal Clues to communicate his needs. List of non-verbal cues:

One snap- Bring your eyes to attention.

Two snaps- Proceed to him with your eyes down and your gaze averted.

Three rapid claps-Find him and wait for directions on what is required of you.

Two fingers straight up- Stop all movement and raise your hands.

Two fingers straight down- Bend over and touch your toes.

One Clap- Follow him.

E. *Secrets are not allowed. If your Dominant discovers anything you did not readily share, it is grounds for immediate termination of the contract.*

F. *Your Dominant does not engage in intercourse, ever. It is the one hard limit that will not be negotiated and is grounds for an immediate contract termination if you try or insist.*

G. *You will remain sexually exclusive with your Dominant, and it is subject, but not limited to kissing, touching, dating, looking, etc. This is to ensure that both parties involved remain free from disease*

You will be required to adhere to all rules placed before you, or it will result in the termination of your contract. Please sign and initial this form along with the Non-Disclosure Agreement attached, and bring them with you to your initial meeting.

X_____

I read the contract thoroughly, twice, and hurriedly grabbed a pen. I signed on the dotted line. The contract was the best news I got all week. I laid down with my heart bursting with excitement. The countdown began now, and that was the last thought I had before I closed my eyes and dreamed of the perfect arrangement.

Chapter 3: Sterling

I was on my way to my youth center, Brilliant Minds, in north Philly. A facility that worked with children who wanted to get a start in the field of information and computer technology. Mentoring the youth was what I loved to do. Today, we were holding presentations for some of our promising students. They would have the opportunity to showcase some of the apps they have been working on completing. It was all in hopes of gaining one of the three grants we had available to take them from idea to development.

I remembered growing up, and the only thing that interested me was books and computer systems. I was the boy who modified all me and my friend's games and even built new levels to some. The only thing was, there were no real programs out to help me expound upon what was working in my mind.

I went to college and developed my first game my freshman year. After that, my career took off. Even after success, I still completed my degree. Five years later, I started my own fortune 500 company. I have been featured in many magazines and articles, although I didn't too much like the limelight. I valued my privacy, and when you become the face of the media, they loved to dissect you and tear you down. A Black man on the rise was a scary thing, but one who used their mind and talents, not only to get ahead, but to bring people up with them, was a downright threat.

I promised myself that I would help as many boys and girls become innovators and make waves in an industry that didn't see many of our faces. I believed that we, as a people, are limitless. The only thing that stood in our way was self-doubt and fear of the power in cooperative economics and community building. I intended to build us back, one young mind at a time. It was never too late to breathe self-awareness and community inside of children.

I parked in my assigned spot and headed inside. When I get in, there was nothing but love to be felt. Children were running up to me in greeting,showing me love, and I gave it right back tenfold. Then, I headed into my office and took a breather before the presentations start.

I was reading emails and checking over inventory when there was a knock on my door. Looking up from my task, I told them to enter. When my door opened, there stood my good friend and frat brother, Maddox Babineaux.

I stood up and came around my desk to happily greet him with a manly hug.

"If it ain't the infamous, Maniac," I said to him when we pulled apart.

"Aww, man, get out of here, Mr. Wet Dream, in da flesh."

I cracked up at him. That damn fool played all day.

"Fuck out of here. I'm glad you could come down and make it as one of the judges. How are you doing, man?" I asked as Maniac took a seat, and we started chatting.

"I'm honored you extended an invite. It's noble what you do here. Be having me feeling all jealous about how my son sings your praises. That's why most of my family, including my wife, is out there to support him for his presentation."

"That's right; you got married and had a new baby. I read the book that dope author did on your love story. *I Love Him But My Soul Craves Another 1 & 2* went hard."

"Yeah, Nadine Frye definitely did our story justice. My wife, Judiyyah, is so dang on shy, but she put her poetry inside of the book to add some extra touches. She

44

had a good time telling our story. We have a beautiful daughter, Abella Adélaïde, and we are happy."

"That's dope, you know I'm happy for you. How you feel about Jr's upcoming presentation?"

His son was my most promising pupil, as well as my Godson. We are trying to teach him about work ethic, and we couldn't do that by just handing him opportunities. So just like every other child at the center, he had to compete for these grants.

"Man, he and his friends have been so secretive about this presentation. He is really taking it to heart that he won't get any special treatment. I can say that he has been working hard. I just hope that it comes across to the panel. I'm not holding any punches. He is a stranger to me today. I hope he came to win."

"Same here. I don't have any picks. I trust that he and the other children are more than prepared."

We spent the next couple of minutes catching up until my secretary announced that it was time to head to the presentation room. When we got inside, we greeted the other judges. In the presentation room, we saw that the families of the presenters were all present. It warmed my heart to see that. Most of the center's children came from broken homes, so to see them surrounded by this type of support lets me know that this program had far-reaching capabilities.

With that pleasant thought in mind, we got right to the presentations, and immediately, I could tell that the presenters had on their game faces. I would not lie, I was absolutely amazed by the work these children put into such astonishing apps. The children didn't know that in addition to the three grand prizes, the runner-up's would each get one-on-one mentoring. It wouldn't just be me mentoring by myself, but a few of my esteemed colleagues in the tech world would be of assistance also.

I was paying attention as my Godson and his friends began their presentation. He and his comrades were confident, and you could tell they came to win. The app they have started developing to counteract bullying was forward-thinking.

They had an interface to match each child with a mentor as well as a group of peers that they could arrange meet and greets. It is so innovative, and I'm a proud papa over here. That is, until Maddox starts grinding my boy up. Maddox was asking him all types of questions from the financial projections to the community benefit of the tech. I was a little tight, but my boy took those questions and presented his data. Maddox Jr. and his friends didn't even break a sweat or flinch. I got proud again, and it was a wrap after that.

Time winded down on the presentations, and it was time to vote. We deliberated, and we were all in agreeance. The judges were more than enthralled with Maddox Jr. and his friends. He didn't take first place but second. They were outshined by a little girl who was seven and created an app for an interactive learning companion for autistic children. That was the fanciest and innovative thing that I had ever seen, and her young mind was one that I would be proud to mold. It lets me know that anything was possible.

We headed out into another conference area to celebrate with the children's families who won the grants. It was a joy to talk with them one-on-one and be congratulatory for their accomplishments, thus fur. When Jr. saw me, he ran up on me, and we engaged in our special handshake. Then, I embraced him and started joking with him.

"GP, what did you think about my presentation?" Maddox Jr. said to me, using the nickname for God Pop he gave me when he was three.

"Young one, it was amazing. I'm more than proud of you, Ty'mir and Xavion. You guys did some impressive work, and it showed in the product you presented. I have no doubt this will take off because this world is affected by bullying," I expressed to him.

"Exactly, GP. We all see the way technology is used as a platform to destroy young lives. Especially on social media, and we want to build up and not destroy any more minds. We had a classmate who committed suicide, and it made us all sad. But we chose to be proactive about it. Even creating a safe space in the school for students to discuss these issues."

Man, when I say proud, I can't even begin to explain how I felt at that moment.

We chopped it up for a little while longer, and I was introduced to Maddox's wife, Judiyyah. She was just gushing over Jr., and their small family looked good.

I was saddened a little, but I quickly shook the feelings off. I may never have what they have, but I would have my perfection in the manner that I chose and could only hope that it would be as fulfilling. Tonight, I shall find out just how perfect for me this new situation would be.

Chapter 4: Anita

My stomach was fluttering relentlessly. I had been a ball of nerves all day thinking about tonight. I had been out all day long, getting prepared for tonight's momentous occasion. Earlier, I went to the spa and got waxed everywhere. I spent time getting a pedicure and manicure and decided to go with a bold red color on my hands and feet. I had my hair in a twist out. These inches are bold, teased out, and all mine.

Nervously, I paced back and forth in my robe, unable to move. I knew I was wearing my carpet out, but I couldn't calm down. I was at a loss on what to wear, and it just seemed like nothing was going right. Uggghh, I was so nervous, and it felt like I might need to shower again. I wanted to make the best impression on him tonight. This opportunity was so significant.I was two seconds away from giving myself heart palpitations.

I heard a knock on my door, so I stopped my musings to respond. My mom entered soon after with boxes and gift bags. When my mom saw the look of distress on my face, she placed the packages on the floor. Opening her arms, she beckoned me to her lovingly. Just like a lost lamb, I ran right into her embrace. There was no comfort like that of a mother.

When we pulled apart, she took my hand and led me over to my bed. We took a seat, and her presence made me instantly calm down.

"What seems to be disturbing your mind, child? I can hear you thinking all the way downstairs."

"Ma, I'm just so bundled up on the inside. It's like, the only thing I ever wanted is here, and now I'm at a loss on what to do. What if he doesn't like me? What if we have no chemistry? I just don't know, mommy. There are so many things that can go wrong." I rushed out my thoughts and then laid my head in my mother's lap.

She gently began to stroke my scalp. It reminded me of the many days I spent in my youth doing this very thing: lying there receiving love and light through her touch.

"Sugar dumpling, you are astonishing, and any dominant would love to have you. You can only be a benefit to his life."

"But, ma, you're just saying that cause I'm your favorite child," I whined in her lap.

"No, baby, I'm not. I love you and your brothers just the same. I'm partial to you being my only daughter, but even more than that, you are just like me. So, I know you are built for this life and all that it entails. You must trust in all that you have lived in and learned in our house. Hopefully, you will find exactly what you most admire in your father and me."

For a few moments longer, I laid in her lap and soaked up her affection. My mother's soothing energy blended with her humming helped the nerves that were racking my body. After she finished comforting me, she quietly laid my head on the bed before exiting my room. Renewed once more, I hopped up to start looking for something to wear when I tripped over something.

When I looked down, I realized it was the boxes and bags my mother had initially brought into me. I picked them up and took a second to admire the pretty packaging. It looked expensive.That made me animated because I loved gifts. I pulled the box out of the biggest package and laid it on the bed. When I opened the lid, I saw a card lying there. There was a scent wafting off of the envelope, and it smelled divine. I open the envelope, and there was a letter inside:

Love,

Today I shall hope to meet perfection

Ready to embrace all my fantasies in the flesh

I hope you are ready for this reality wrapped in
desires.

Your body, mind, and soul are mine to capture.

I hope you are ready to be captivated!

-Your New Proprietor

P.S. Inside this box, you will find all you need to
greet me tonight. I can't wait to unwrap my gift. Be outside
of your address at promptly 6:45 P.M.

That note gave me a renewed sense of energy. Just hearing from him had given me just what I needed to be confident about tonight. I unwrapped the paper from the box, and inside there was an outfit with a mask on top. Removing the mask to see the outfit, I burst out into a fit of giggles. The outfit had my personality all over it.

This red and black latex romper would showcase my best asset, and that was my ass. I didn't have much in the boob department, but this ass was more than a handful. I laid the outfit out on the bed and surveyed the mask. It was reminiscent of *The Phantom of the Opera*, as it would only cover the right side of my face. The mask was an intricately designed Venetian masquerade mask. It was infused with rubies and rhinestones, so I knew I would feel beyond sexy once I placed it on.

I dug inside of the bag again and pulled out a long box. When I opened it, I swear I was in love. Inside was a pair of thigh-high boots that laced up and had a peep-toe. I remove my robe and began getting dressed with vigor.

When I slid the romper on, it clung to my curves. The center of the romper over my breast was oval cut. It pushed my perky, B-cup breasts together, giving me some deep cleavage action. I sat down on the side of the bed and started to put on my shoes. I laced the boots upon my thighs, then stood to go survey the look in my full-length mirror.

My reflection showed me that I was ready and so prepared to play. I grabbed the mask and placed it on my face. The mask made me feel dramatic and complimented my Red Ombre, special effect lip I decided to go with today.

My face was beat, check.

My ass sat high and jiggled, check.

My ride was on the way, and now it was time to go.

When I made it outside, I was right on time. Damn, that ride looked smooth and presented wealth. It was a Dodge, LA Custom Coach Black Dodge Challenger SRT 8. The color was bold and put you in a playful frame of mind. I came down the steps, and the driver was waiting valiantly at the bottom of the steps. As soon as my foot touched the last stair, the chauffeur grabbed my hand and led me to the door. Before I stepped inside of the car, he handed me a letter.

Accepting the envelope, I step inside the car. To my surprise, I was met with five other ladies. All of whom were beautiful and blessed with copious amounts of melanin in different shades and perfections. I spoke, and my eyes were immediately drawn to this chocolate beauty near the window. She looked regal in her royal blue and black. I was here for that. Once I was seated comfortably, I opened my letter and proceeded to read.

Ms. Fox,

Tonight, you embark on a new journey. Your Dom has only been given preliminary info about you. He does not know your name or have any idea who you are, so it will be up to you to make an excellent first impression. You and the other ladies have all been provided a number.

Yours is 5. When you enter the mansion, you ladies should line up left to right according to your number. This will be how you will identify who it is that will own you. Make tonight one to remember.

Well, what a warm welcome to our new lives. We were only driving for a short while when we pulled up to a familiar home. I was overcome with excitement because my best friend Ta'iah stood outside of her residence, and she looked scrumptious. When she entered the car, she didn't automatically notice my presence. As soon as she did, you would think we didn't just see each other yesterday the way she jumped all over me.

"Oh my God, Anita, I thought I would only see you on the inside of the club," Ta'iah said to me.

When she pulled back, I had a chance to see she was looking cute in her little tutu ensemble.

"Yasssss, best friend! Look at you! Slay-yyy bitch," I told her while snapping my fingers and twerking in my seat.

"This car is nice and cozy."

"Yes, and the amenities are nice. Did you read your note yet?"

"No. So everybody got notes?" Ta'iah asked the car's occupants.

We all nodded our heads, yes, and she sat back to open the note. She read it, placed it back in the envelope, then turns to me.

"So, what is your number?" she asked.

"I'm number 5, and you?"

"I'm number 4 so you will be to my right. Who will be to my left?"

"That would be me, lucky number 3."

The chocolate beauty by the window raised her hand and replied. I saw Ta'iah have a slightly gay moment as she gazed long at her. I mean, if you could see the magnificence radiating off her obsidian skin, you might ponder switching teams as well. They could bottle her smooth chocolate skin and get rich off that gold.

"Hi, I'm Ta'iah, and you are beautiful," my bestie introduced herself, a little star-struck.

"Thank you! I'm Zahra, and you're looking like a snack yourself."

Just like that, the atmosphere relaxed as we began to network and talked amongst ourselves. I was amazed to find out Zahra created the outfits we all wore that night. We were excited to meet someone like-minded. We told her how we created most of the pieces that will be used in our play at the club, and we hoped everyone enjoyed them. We talked and exchanged numbers, and before we knew it, we were pulling up outside of the club.

My nerves began running amuck in my belly. Knowing that inside of that grand-looking space could be the manifestation of my hopes and dreams was overwhelming. Anxious and excited, I began thinking about how my Dom would look and how well we would fit. The possibilities were endless, and I was finally ready just as Ta'iah spoke.

"Okay, ladies, its showtime."

With that statement, we filed out of the car. I put my game face on. It was time to meet my destiny.

Chapter 5: Sterling

Today was the day I meet my lady, and I expected to feel some type of trepidation. Surprisingly, I had been as cool as the other side of a pillow. Meticulously, I took my time getting ready for tonight. I decided to go with a classic man look to set the tone for my love. The blazer I wore was red velvet with a black trim. The shirt was black, as well as my pants which were tailored to perfection. I paired my look with a pair of Gucci loafers and a red bowtie.

Tonight was about more than me finding a woman to subjectify. Tonight, I intended to possibly make a match with someone that would meet my needs forever. I wanted someone who would let me open up their mind to a life that exceeded sex and its raunchiness. I'd been searching for someone willing to submit their mind to a new plateau that I could create for us and live there indefinitely.

My greatest hope was that she could live life without sex and understand that it held no basis in our utopia. I needed a woman who could think outside of two bodies slapping together for a few moments and allow me to open her eyes to the newness of intimacy. There were so many ways for people to connect, especially if we could only use the quieted recesses of our brain to reach nirvana.

I hopped in my Tesla and headed out to the club. I was so happy for my good friend Dominant. He had been trying to open this club since we all had been on the scene together. Our other best friend, Zuri, and I had been encouraging him to do something different than what we were used too. That was all Dominant needed to build us a sanctuary that adequately catered to our needs.

When we were coming up on the scene, most of the places that served the purpose for Dominant/Submissive liaisons were whole in the walls. They were places that offered little in the way of discretion or options. Those clubs didn't particularly cater to the proclivities of Black men. BDSM was a thing you only heard of being native to Caucasians with a weird sense of kink. It made us feel on the outside since we knew that our people loved the life just as much. So, this club paid homage to Black men who loved to think outside the box when it came to their agreements.

I pulled through the wrought iron gates, and the only thing I could think was that Dominant really put his money where his mouth was. I mean, everything about the venue screamed lavish, luxurious, and grandiose. I parked my car and headed up the stairs. Bending down, I had my face scanned for access.

When I stepped inside, my mouth dropped in awe. Dominant was on some otherworld stuff. To men with specific tastes, this extra security measure was a bonus. When you came to play, the last thing you want to worry about is someone with ill intentions getting in and exposing you to the world. The high tech touch lets you know that what you do privately is just that.

When I walked into the foyer, it was like Christmas time, and I was instantly inspired. There were pretty little brown bunnies walking around and serving guests, and I'd never been more proud to be blessed with melanin. The color scheme was inviting and put you in the mindset to get a little risqué. I headed over to what appeared to be a man cave on steroids.

When I saw all of the gentlemen there, it was like being back in my frat days. There were all different shades of Black men sitting around politicking. Some men were enjoying the comforts of the women provided for the occasion. Some were having drinks with a nice cigar and conversation. It was such a sight to behold, and I was ready to join the festivities. I locked eyes with my homie

Dominant and headed in his direction just as he was heading into mine.

"Dominant, my main-man, what's going on?" I greeted him as soon as we got close. Then we embraced in a manly hug and started playing catch up with each other.

"Sterling, it's always great to see my folks."

"This is amazing. Watching your dream finally come together is ethereal," I complimented Dominant on his efforts because, indeed, it was. The attention he paid to detail was beyond any of our wildest dreams.

"Yeah, it is wonderous. I never thought this would be anything but a dream."

"I never doubted that you would, and it is pure genius. Now I can't wait to see if your team got our selections right." I rubbed my hands together in anticipation.

"I hope no one will be disappointed, myself included. The team that chose the girls took the job very seriously concerning the selection," Dominant told me as if he was trying to alleviate my fears with that disclaimer.

"I have faith in you, but I'm just anxious to meet mine," I told him honestly.

Shit, I was more than a little anxious about meeting a complete stranger. It was scary. I hoped she would meet my standards and came with a willingness to comply.

"Me too, and I hope she is perfect. You know how these women say they about that life until it's time to show and prove."

"Yeah, men with our proclivities are hard to please, and you, sir, are insufferable."

Out of all of us, Dominant's demands were enough to make grown men blush, but I could respect his needs.

"Sterling, get out of here. Let's bust it up about business real quick. The girls should be arriving shortly, and I intend to be busy."

We talked about how he wanted to start getting more involved in my community center. Dominant's ideas could work if we put the right people in place. I told him that he should possibly think of opening up a center that focused on music and art. Our little boys and girls didn't have enough programs that enriched their culture or their minds. The waves Dominant and his brother were making in the industry were nothing less than phenomenal. They could definitely go a long way to advancing the youth in the inner city. Like George Tandy Jr. said, "Music saves the kids."

We were interrupted by the arrival of our other best friend, Zuri Williams. Zuri stood there looking ethnic as fuck as he was rocking Dashiki colors with a curly fro-hawk. We embraced him, and he jumped right into our conversation. Zuri was the man with the numbers. He handled our finances on top of being one of the biggest acquisitionist we knew.

If he wasn't my best friend, I might have been concerned because Zuri was known to take over companies. But he had the Midas touch, and any company he took over, he molded into a multi-million conglomerate.

"So, what's with the numbers that we were given?" Zuri asked Dominant.

His inquiry made me remember the note and number I received before I arrived.

"My manager said that's how we will realize which girl is ours. We are supposed to line up from right to left according to the numbers we were given."

That was a pretty creative way of introduction.

"Well, what number did you get?" Zuri asked Dominant

"I got four, and you?" He responded back

"I got three, and what about you, Sterl?" Zuri asked me.

"I got five," I replied to them

"Man, that's wild. Three the hard way even while we play!" Zuri exclaimed.

I laughed at that expression. Man, some of the things we have gotten into together. Those were stories for another day, though.

"You already know. What do you guys plan on doing as an introduction to your lady?" Dominant asked us.

"Man, I want to see if she can take the pain. That is important to me, and we won't have anything to discuss if she can't weather the storm I'm going to bring to her," Zuri responded to Dominant, and I understood his passion.

"Well, I want to see if my girl can play in a fantasy setting. I plan to test her ability to adapt at the drop of a hat. And what about you, Dominant?" I told my guys because a mind was a terrible thing to waste. I needed her mind to be at its fullest capacity to live in my zone

"I haven't decided yet, but I want to see how well we mesh. I will take my kitten through a few paces and rely on her cues to tell me where to lead her next," Dominant told us.He'd always been one to wing it and bring it together.

I looked down at my watch and saw that it was about that time.

"Well, fellas, it's time we made it out to the foyer and met these ladies."

We headed into the foyer, and it was not just my bros and me alone. Four other gentlemen were lining up with us. Dominant stood at the center, and I was to his left with Zuri to his right. We formed a sort-of open-ended triangle.

At exactly 7:45 P.M., the doors opened, and in walked the most splendid sight I had ever seen. So much beauty walked through the front door, and I could speak for the other gentlemen when I said we were captivated. The ladies lined up and mirrored our formation. When I locked eyes with the beauty that was mine, she automatically averted her gaze. Her posture was alert but relaxed. Submission never looked better on an individual than it did on her.

My lady was all wild hair, long legs, and obedience. The subservience in her aura drew me in like a moth in a flame. I couldn't wait to get to the room and commune with her one on one. I saw Dominant escort his lady out, and I could wait no more. I stepped forward and snapped my fingers once, and her eyes clicked straight to mine. I saw so many emotions in their depths. The most prominent one was willingness. I turned away from her and clapped once. I didn't bother looking behind me because I was sure she was right on my trail.

I led her straight to the top floor, where my room was just off to the right of the staircase. When I opened the door, I stood back and let her inside the room. When she walked inside, I saw her stop and look around. My lady was probably confused since I had the room revamped for this particular night. Let us see if she could complete the first challenge.

Chapter 6: Anita

When I walked into the mansion turned club with Ta'iah in lead of us girls, I was intrigued. When we got inside, our men were standing in formation. As reflections of them, we followed their lead. When I looked to see who was standing in front of my place in line, I couldn't stare for too long.

He was magnificent. My Dom was light-skinned with honey-colored eyes and the cutest birthmark on his face. He was tall and fit, and his grown man look was turning me on. It had me wanting to pledge my allegiance to his kingdom. A man in a suit always did it for me because it showed that they were serious about their business. Nothing made a girl swoon harder than a man that donned a perfectly tailored outfit.

I quickly averted my gaze and automatically got inside of my head.

Will I be able to do this? Will this end like all the other times?

I didn't even have the time to think before my first command was given. That snap authorized my gaze to his attention. Then, he turned around and clapped once before walking away.

Like a sheep that's led out to pasture, I followed him. As I walked behind that magnificent specimen, it felt like an honor. Up the stairs, we went until we reached a door just to the right of the staircase. He unlocked the door and allowed me to enter before him, and the splendor of the room rendered me speechless.

When I stepped inside the room, it felt like I was transported to an island. The black, green, and yellow flags, indicative of Jamaica, flew proudly. They were placed strategically around the room. It smelled as if he brought the ocean right inside of our chamber. The atmosphere was fragrant, and I swore that I could taste the salt of the sea on my tongue.

There was a table set up, and you could smell aromatic spices flowing off of the dishes. The scent of the food was enticing my stomach to rumble.My goodness, that would be embossing and so unladylike.

There was a hammock in the middle of the room held up by faux coconut trees. Maybe they were real. I couldn't see him to be inauthentic to the moment. I stood there, wound tighter than a coil waiting for further instruction. He walked to the table, removed his blazer, and then placed it on the back of the chair.

He rolled up the sleeves of his dress shirt which gave him a more relaxed look. As relaxed as he appeared, his aura still felt heavy. I was poised and ready for him to command me. He began walking towards me, and my heart rate rapidly sped up. His magnificence entered my personal space, and he just perused me. From head to toe as if taking inventory. His gaze was as intimate as any caress.

He reached his hands up to my face and gently removed the mask. I instantly felt exposed. His face bore a sexy smirk as he lifted my chin and tilted my head back until our eyes became deadlocked. I knew he could hear my breath hitch to match the frenzy his scrutiny caused my heart. Gazing into his eyes was intense, and I became unsteady on my feet. He grabbed me by my arms and began to rub them soothingly.

"Relax, love. All is well when you are in my presence. No need for you to panic because you are safe," he assured me.

I could only nod my head to indicate I understood. Being that close to him hadmomentarily turned me into a mute. All of my senses seemed to have left me. He gave me a beaming smile before he spoke to me again.

"Let me introduce myself. I'm Sterling, and you may address me as any pet name in which you feel comfortable. I'm not rigid enough to have you calling me, Sir. What I intend is to create a dalliance with a foundation of mutual respect. I want you to feel comfortable with me and my direction as if you can breathe in my guidance and exhale its appropriate obedience. I don't rule with a firm hand, but I will punish disobedience and reward your good behavior. Is this okay with you?"

I nodded my head to which he reached down to pinch me harshly on my thigh.

"I need you to answer me verbally when I address you directly. Do you understand everything I have said to you, love?" Sterling asked me again.

"Yes, honey, I do understand."

"Very good. Does perfection have a name?" he asked me, and it made me giggle coquettishly at his compliment.

"Yes, it's Anita."

"Hmmm...it's meaning is grace, and God has favored me. Staring at the sight before me, I have to agree that I am highly favored," he said while sliding his hand down my frame.

It turned my body feverishly hot.

"Thank you," I responded to his compliment in a whisper.

"No need to thank me yet, but before the end of the night, your gratitude will be more than deserving. Do you have your contract?"

I reached inside my romper and pulled the contract out of my bra. He took it from my hand and sniffed the paper. That action made my vagina constrict as if Sterling sniffed me personally. He opened our agreement and studied it for a moment before he then placed it on the table. My eyes knitted in confusion.

Why didn't he sign the contract?

That made me start to panic. I was feeling bewildered and overtly anxious. It must have been plastered on my face when he turned around to me.

He invaded my personal space, runninghis hand through my hair. That precious caress caused the muscles in my face and body to relax. Sterling's touch was very comforting, and my errant heart calmed once more. He pulled back until our eyes connected.

"No need to be alarmed.love. I know you're probably wondering why I didn't sign the contract. I have only one test for you to pass before I happily sign it. This step is crucial to me, as it is how I govern my life. I want to be able to take your mind and soul and give them a cohesive existence.

What we will hopefully do will exceed the physical, although, at times, it will be one of the vehicles we use to reach new heights. The body is the exception and not the rule to what we will experience together. I want you to go into the bathroom, and your next set of instructions will be waiting for you. You think you can handle this challenge, love?"

"I believe that I can, sugar," I said with certainty.

"That's what I like to hear. Let the night begin."

With that encouragement, I headed off into the bathroom. There was an outfit laid out on the counter with accessories to match on top. I headed over to the counter to get a good look at the items. There was an envelope sitting right on top of my wares. Shakily, I grabbed the note and opened it up. I took the slip of paper out and began reading.

Love,

Tonight, you and I are strangers on a beautiful tropical Island. The thing about strangers is that they are not bound by any pressures to be something they are not.

On this island, thousands of miles from life, reality, and responsibilities, you can be whomever your heart desires. I am nobody but can be your everything. No judgments or preconceived notions. Show me who you are.

I think I could imagine exactly where this test was going. Sterling had given me a prime opportunity to show him my versatility. I wrapped my mind around the note and put myself exactly where I needed to be, mentally, in order to execute his instructions. I began to undress out of the black and red short romper. I removed my shoes, and picked up the dress that was on the counter.

Slipping it on my body, I loved the way that the neckline plunged and gave a flattering peek at my B-cup breast and flat tummy. The bottom flared but had splits that reached up to my waistline. This dress was the type that gave off the flirty dramatic effect that said I'm classy but a little risqué. I looked into the mirror and saw that my Ombre lip, nor the beat face, went with the desired look.

I grabbed a facial towel and began to remove my makeup. Once my face was thoroughly clean, I grabbed the Shea Butter on the counter. I took a liberal amount of it into my palm, rubbed my hands together, and applied it to my face, neck, and arms.

There was a little caddy with makeup options, and since the Shea Butter gave my face a natural glow, I decided to do the minimum. Grabbing the stick of eye kohl, I thicklyoutlined my irises. Going with the cat-eye look for a dramatic effect, I made sure the lining was dark and bold. I chose a light pink lip glass from M.A.C. to slather my unlined lips and puckered up to make sure it was even.

The accessories were beautifully chosen to compliment my dress. There were bangles of silver with black beads and jade stones throughout them with earrings to match. I loved my hair wild and free, but for the accessories to really pop, I had to tame my mane. I parted my tresses down the middle and began to place two loose French braids in the front of my hair. I secured the braid with some bobby pins and allowed the tail end to flair into my curls.

Staring in the mirror, I took in my look. I was happy with the results. I looked like someone who was relaxed and allowing the island to relieve my stress. I decided that my shoes don't go with the island feel, so I chose to go barefoot in my ensemble.

Everything that I wanted in life was just beyond that door. I had to remember I trained my whole existence for this moment. Failure was not an option for me, and I didn't come to leave without my dreams. I grabbed the knob of the door and stopped to take a deep breath. When I turned the knob to open the door, I was in the zone. Sterling was what I wanted, and he was what I would have.

Chapter 7: Sterling

I was laid inside of the hammock, just rocking mindlessly. My thoughts were about the lovely specimen of a woman that I had been paired with. They ran amuck as she readied herself for me in the bathroom. Anita's brown eyes are were doe-like, bright, and inviting. The type of peepers one got lost inside of if they gazed too long. Her aura screamed innocence, but, in her gaze, there was a fire. A fire that called out,"Consume me, show me, and use me."

I intended to do all of those things, and so much more.

I was a little nervous about the rest of the night. By her first impression, I desired to keep her, but if she couldn't pass my test, I would not need her. People generally felt like role play was low on the totem pole of BDSM, but for me, it was a way of life. I needed a woman that was as fluent as language. If I changed the game at the drop of a hat, she needed to be on her toes enough to quickly adapt.

What I had planned for her tonight was something on the small end of the spectrum, but it was a test, nontheless. I wanted to see if she would come out of the bathroom the same way she went in, and I'm not just talking physically. If my instructions, although vague, forced her to use her intelligence, then I would be able to see it in her character. This was a moment where I deciphered if I could meet her at the mind.

There was some calypso music playing in the background, lending authenticity to the scene. Although the music was upbeat, it was also soothing and put your mind at ease. The chords in the beat touched your limbs and made you relax.

Anita had been in the bathroom for a little minute, so I hoped I didn't scare her away. She went in with optimism, so it was no way she would miss the opportunity. If I read her right, Anita loved a challenge. I closed my eyes with a smile, thinking about how determined she appeared when I presented the challenge to her. The intensity in her eyes was almost defiant, and I hoped she keeps that same fire.

The sound of a door opening greeted my ears. I turned around, and by God, Anita looked delicious. The dress and jewelry I'd chosen draped her with perfection. She didn't even look my way as she headed over to the buffet I had set up in the room. I watched the Africa in her hips bounce from side-to-side like a drum beat. It was like they were inviting me in a siren's song to reach out and touch. Her movements left me mesmerized, and I didn't want to wake up.

I felt a stirring in my loins, and that seldomly happened. I was usually able to handle the opposite sex with a calm aloofness unless *I* invited the desire. It took years for me to control my body, and it generally only acted on my command. But just watching Anita was causing me to feel as if my temple was malfunctioning.

She proceeded to place various items on her plate from the buffet. The whole time her hips were moving to the beat of the music that played in the background. Once she finished, I saw her looking around. I thought she was looking for me until her eyes focused on the table and lit up. Anita made her way to the table, where she gracefully seated herself.

She crossed her beautiful legs, and the split in the dress showed off her toned thighs. Even while she ate daintily, Anita was magnificent to behold. I loved the way she took the time to savor her food as if each bite was a delicacy. Her eyes were closed, and Anita's face bore a look that rivaled one filled with orgasmic bliss.

Then, the minx placed another forkful of rice in her mouth, and my tumescence elongated in my pants. The way she wrapped her tongue around that fork to make sure she caught everything blew my mind. It was the sexiest shit I had ever witnessed. I never wanted to be a utensil as bad as I did at that moment.

I sat up in the hammock because she held my complete attention. Now, I was ready for this game to begin. I got up and sauntered my way over to Anita's table. As soon as I stood in front of her, I spoke.

"Good evening, beautiful. Would you mind a little company to go with your meal and a beautiful starry night?"

Anita brought her eyes up to mine before perusing me from head to toe. Her introspective surveying made me feel like a meal she planned to devour.

"Your company sounds like a wonderful addition. Please, have a seat."

I took the seat she offered right across from her. Once comfortable, I'd started scrutinizing the beautiful specimen before me. Anita had removed her makeup, and even bare-faced, her beauty couldn't be denied. She had a natural glow that made her brown skin appear luminous.

Her lips were full, pouty, and covered in a pink-tinted lip-gloss that made me want to partake of their fullness.

I noticed her hair was not as full as before when we first met. The new, casual hairstyle drew my attention to her captivating face, and I couldn't remove my gaze. For endless minutes, my eyes devoured her elegance.

"Do you intend to stare at me as if you're lost in the greatest story ever written, or will you provide me with the companionship you offered?"

Anita's question brought me out of my trance.

"Oh, she is witty, I see. Why is a lovely being such as yourself having the most intimate meal of the day alone?"

"Being as though I came to this island alone, and I must eat, I decided to leave the confines of my room. I wanted to have my food while enjoying nature and all its mysteries. What about yourself? I noticed you are in this fine establishment with no adornments on your arm."

"No, I have no one with me. I came to the island to clear my head and study the people for an upcoming book I have in the works. I've been trying to see if the natives will inspire my creativity."

"Wow, that is fascinating. I've never met an author before. What type of books do you write?" she probed for more.

"I mainly write erotica/erotic poetry," I responded to her inquiry.

"Hmmm, that seems very interesting. You create foreplay through verbiage. I wonder how many late nights you have inspired through your stories."

The last part I believe was rhetorical, but I caught none the less and respond.

"I like to think I have inspired many to elevate their understanding of lovemaking. My stories tend to push the boundaries of one's imagination. Making fantasy and reality correlate so closely that it changes perception. Perception is the key to all matters of intimacy. Taking your senses and immersing them inside of another to derive the satisfaction of ecstasy. So, I hope I don't just inspire late nights, but a better way for people to obtain an understanding of their partner through the mind. Which the body becomes the vehicle to get them to their destination."

I said a mouthful while staring intensely into Anita's eyes. She sat at the edge of her seat, hanging on to my every word. Her lips were parted slightly as her breathing hitched, and her pupils dilated. It appeared my words sent Anita into another zone. She shook her head, and then her eyes focused back on me as if she was rejoining me back in this realm.

"Are you hungry?" She huskily asked.

"I could eat."

Anita hopped up out of her seat as if it was on fire. On unsteady feet, as if she was in mid-swoon, she headed over to the buffet to make me a plate. I watched as Anita subtly used her hand to fan her face. She then grabbed her dress to, I assume, fan her lady parts.

I was turned on watching the evidence of what my words were doing to her body. Anita was doing better than I expected her to in this scenario. And on bare feet, which was a plus because it meant she was unafraid to be comfortable. Anita showed me she needn't waste time overly dressing in this relaxed atmosphere, and I dug her vibe.

After a moment of effectively making my plate, Anita came and placed it before me, along with a ginger beer. I noticed that she had given me a plate that was proportioned correctly—giving me a sample of everything the buffet had to offer. My stomach involuntarily rumbled at the smell of the delicious meal. The sight of the eye-appetizing meal made me remember that I had not eaten all day in anticipation of our meeting.

"Thank you for the plate, as well as fixing it for me. Those types of manners speak volumes." I rewarded her with an honest compliment.

"It was no trouble at all. I want you to feel welcome in my presence," she responded with kindness.

Anita then took her seat. We ate and held a fantastic conversation. We discussed life and every facet of the world we lived in. I switched topics often to see if she could keep up with me and my thought process. Anitadid more than kept up. She impressed me with her knowledge and understanding of my conversational selections. We laughed and even flirted to the point it skirted on the improper. Before I knew it, we had finished our meal.

Although we only discussed surface things, I still felt as though we were connecting. I got to know Anita a little better with the small glimpses she gave me of herself. I was able to see that she was gentle, confident, intelligent, and subservient. Our conversation, and how she adapted to this moment, made my decision to keep her quite easy—as long as she passes this last test.

It's a small one but something I remembered and applied to my ideals. It was a southern etiquette, one that not many women knew, but I expected *mine* to be aware. I headed over to the buffet, grabbed a small plate, and placed some sliced fruit upon its surface. When I made it back to the table, I moved my chair beside hers and took a seat while placing the plate between us.

"After such an enlightening conversation, I thought we should have a little dessert and continue. Would you like to have some fruit?"

"That is a great idea. I would love to have some."

I picked up the fork and impale a slice of pineapple. I lifted the fork to Anita's lips, and she moved her head back. She smiled at me demurely before saying, "Where I'm from, if a man offers you food, you should eat it from his fingertips."

Anita spoke so innocently, as if she didn't want to offend me. It was the sexiest shit I ever heard from a subject. I was glad to say she had officially passed my test. I dropped the fork and began feeding her the fruit until it was all gone. It became a forbidden dance of me feeding her, licking juices from her chin and lips as she coyly accepted all of my advances.

Anita never pushed the limits, nor did she ask for more. She just allowed me to take as much as I wanted and basked in the leadership I offered. Anita did that all the while soaking in the attention I doted on her like a good girl.

When the fruit was gone, I stood up and headed back into the general area of the room. Anita was sitting there watching me, and I could see uncertainty in her gaze. I snapped my fingers twice. She stood right up and came to stand in front of me with her head bowed and gaze averted. I loved the submission in her stance. I snapped once, and her head snapped up, but her gaze was a bit unsure. I smiled at her brightly to alleviate her fears.

"My dearest, Anita. I want to tell you that I'm proud and beyond pleased at your behavior. You have shown me tonight that you will exceed all of my expectations. I'm glad to tell you that I will sign the contract and take you home with me. In my home is where I will do my absolute best to lead you, teach you, protect you, and make your mind the best part of your anatomy. How does that make you feel?"

"It is an honor to be chosen, and I will make this the best decision you ever made," she said as a tear slipped out her eye and down her cheek.

I wiped her tears as she rubbed her face along my palm. Such an affectionate little bird. I pulled back and placed my hand out to her. Anita grasped my hand with all of the trust inside of her. I accepted her acquiescence. Then, I led her back out through the club and into the beginning of our story.

The beginning of the end...

Chapter 8: Anita

Sunlight signals new beginnings
A new day brings endless possibilities
Today, we start a path that is a blank canvas
What we create, will rival the creation of the fallen Mayan
temples
Mornings are the best time to get to know yourself
Also, it's the best time to show gratitude for the blessing of life
Don your robe and meet me downstairs in the second room to
the left of the stairs
Your reawakening awaits.
-Your new beginning

It is the first morning after our meeting at the club, and Sterling's note had me excited. Last night, he brought me back to his dwelling, located in a secluded suburb of Wynnefield. It was humungous and built like a secluded cabin. Equipped with open-spaced concepts and too many rooms to count, it was magnificent. Immediately, I noticed the wrap-around staircase, the modern appliances, and how the house looked and smelled like home.

Sterling's tour led us upstairs where he showed me to our living quarters. Initially, when we arrived, I'd assumed that Sterling would put me into a room designed just for me. But, he shocked me when he told me that we would share every space inside of the home harmoniously.

Sterling's reasoning was that to build an unshakeable bond: we needed to connect through sharing time, space, and conversation.

Our bedroom ended the tour but didn't end our connection. Sterling gave me such a sensual night that had left a lasting impression. It also reaffirmed that my decision to live this life was correct. We started with a shared bath where he cleansed me from head to toe while we listened to jazz instrumentals. We went from the bath to our room, where Sterling massaged me from head to toe with coconut oil blended with vanilla and cinnamon. His hands felt like those of a potter molding their latest creation as my muscles were the clay.

After the massage, Sterling dressed me in a nightgown. Spun from the most beautiful silk that melted against my skin, it made me feel like royalty. Then, we both laid down for bed where he held me close as we kissed and conversed with one another. It was a beautiful night. One that ended with him cuddling me as he told me a story that rivaled many fairytales I'd heard growing up. I went to sleep feeling cherished and as if I belonged to Sterling in every way that mattered. For the first time in my adult life, I understood intimacy on an elemental level.

Now, after receiving his note, I was abuzz with excitement to see what our morning held. Following Sterling's instructions, I made my way downstairs to the room he desired to meet. When I made it into the room, I gasped audibly.

The room was like a forest oasis. Vines went from one end of the room to the other, sporting various fragrant flowers. Automatically, I inhaled, and my senses were overtaken with the fresh and serene scent. A garden tub laid in the middle of the floor, and Sterling stood on its side. He was shirtless and barefoot with pajama bottoms slung low on his hips; a towel draped over his arm. I deeply blushed as he stood there, looking like a blessing in the physical form that set my hormones ablaze.

"Good morning, love. How are you feeling today?" Sterling asked me huskily.

His tone caressed me like warm honey.

"Morning, sugar. I am doing good, and you?"

"You most certainly look it. I'm great love. I've been up for the last few hours, preparing your morning stimulation and relaxation. Come to me."

My feet carried me over to him like a puppet master pulling strings. When I stood in front of him, Sterling pulled me close and wrapped me in his arms. Automatically, I held him back and melted into his embrace as if we had naturally done this many mornings before. Sterling started petting my neck and my nose. He inhaled my scent which made my spine tingle, and I pulled him in closer. His nose replaced his tongue at my neck. Involuntarily, my walls clenched tightly, and my essence released down my thighs as my knees weakened. Sterling caught me right before I fell. As he held me in his arms, my eyes lowered in discomfiture. He stood me back on my feet

"Such a responsive beauty. Did you make a mess of yourself?" Sterling asked me, and that made me feel dirty.

"Yes," I whispered with embarrassment. I couldn't believe that I had an orgasm just off of his simple touches.

"Don't be shy, love. It makes me happy to provide you pleasure. It all works for the atmosphere that I intend to build in our new world. I was so impressed with you last night that I woke up this morning, hoping to strengthen the connection we began. You are the newest edition to my life, and I want you to know that I intend to make you comfortable here in every aspect *of my life*.

What I want to build is a life filled with stability and happiness. You are not here to only serve my needs,

91

although your subjugation resonates within my soul and has become a new form of oxygen. I want you to understand that your needs are equally important, and it will become my life's undertaking to make sure your needs are fulfilled. Now, let me undress you and soothe your mind."

Ever so gently, Sterling removed my robe, trailing his fingertips butterfly soft over my skin—raising the gooseflesh in response to the sensory overload. Taking my hand, he led me into the garden tub. The water bordered on steaming and immediately soothed my muscles when I stepped inside. I sat down, and once I rested, I exhaled. On my inhale, my senses overran with mint, lemon verbena, and grapefruit.

"Lay your head back, love." I did as he requested and felt the lethargy taking over me instantly. "Now, close your eyes and don't open them again until I tell you too."

My eyes snapped shut. I could hear and feel everything in amplification. It took everything in me to keep my eyes closed, but I complied in hopes of being rewarded for my obedience. The soft sounds of Kem's "I'm in Love" played melodically in the background, and I felt the music down to my toes.

The whole package of the heavenly feeling water, the music, and the smell of the atmosphere had me almost comatose. The soft downy touch of a feather slid from behind my ear to around my neck. It tickled at first until Sterling ran the feather across my nipple, that sat just atop of the water, and they puckered to a peak. Around and around, he swirled the feather until I was crossing my legs, and my breathing became choppy.

"Breathe, love. Inhale and exhale and just feel the vibe," Sterling instructed me as he continued his torture on my overly sensitive bosom.

I was squirming by the time he dragged the feather gently across my collarbone. Suddenly, the feeling stopped and was replaced with the warmth of his hand. Sterling began kneading my nipple with his smooth fingertips. It was like he had bolts in their tips as my body became electrified with passion. Then, both hands were working overtime, and the sensations had me grabbing the side of the tub.

One hand began to run down the front of my body as his other hand worked my nipples with precision. When Sterling's hand disappeared underwater and brushed over my flower, my heart stopped for a few beats.

"Spread your legs a little, love," Sterling whispered in my ear.

My thighs spread, and Sterling peeled my petals back. He began to rub my bud languidly. It felt as if Sterling was composing music the way he was directing my nectar to drip from my flower and blend with the fragrant water of the tub. Mewls and coos were escaping my lips. Right before tension started in my toes and rapidly begqn to rise through my limbs.

"That's right, love, purr for me. I feel you vibrating as I strum your pearl. It's okay to let go. Let me feel your love rain down."

That was all it took for me to surrender to a cataclysmic orgasm. One that paralyzed my heart and vocals for seconds. Like yarn, I unraveled. Sterling guided my unleashing with his relentless strokes and verbal encouragement. After the last quake left my body, I ly in the tub, feeling like unmolded putty. My eyelids were drooping as my head lolled to the side.

"No time for resting, love. Stand so that I can wash you. I only have one question. How do you feel?"

"Happy," I responded with no hesitation.

"That was my goal."

I stood, and Sterling meticulously washed me from head to toe, twice. He wrapped me in a fluffy towel, then took my hand and led me to the table. Once we were seated, Sterling began to feed me a breakfast that consisted of oatmeal with dates, raisins, and apples. There was also eggs and toast. In between bites, he kissed me, gazed into my eyes, touched my exposed, and told me of my beauty.

I'd only ever been doted on by my parents. To have Sterling lavishing me with affection and care was overwhelming. I cried some, but they were tears of happiness. Our morning communion was a perfect start to our dalliance. It gave me hope for the future that held for our new life.

It has been two weeks since I've brought Anita home. I can say it was one of the best decisions of my life. She fit my world in more ways than I could imagine. I came home every day to a home-cooked meal and a smile that melted my heart. For so many years, outside of my friends, I lived a solitary existence. Now, I looked forward to coming home.

Today, I had been working from home and preparing for Anita to get in from work. I have a new technique I wanted to introduce her to. I texted her earlier to take a shower and meet me in the darkroom. Tonight, I wanted to blow her mind. I stood from my office chair and proceeded to our bedroom. The scent of lemongrass met me once I opened the door. The aroma always soothed me, and it was that unique touch that Anita provided since she made my house a home.

I'd already showered, but I needed to grab the candles I stored in my drawer. After collecting the candles, I headed downstairs to the darkroom. This particular room had never been utilized because I'd been studying the perfect type of environment to set. I've been interested in Tantric sex for years. It involves various erotic activities, and not all involve penetration or physical stimulation of erogenous zones. Tantric sex, most times, include the subtle dimensions of slow embraces, gentle caresses, becoming present within the body, and focusing on the movement of energy between the partners' bodies.

As I dimmed the lights, I lit the various tropical scented candles all around the room. Once done with that task, I turned the sounds of nature on low so that it would become the white noise in the background. I removed my pajama bottoms and proceeded to sit in the circle of candles upon a throw pillow. As soon as I was seated, there was a timid knock on the door.

"You may enter," I called out to Anita, and swiftly, she entered the room.

Anita stood before me, a vision of beauty that radiated outwards. The beatific smile upon her face always shook me to my core. No matter what she encountered outside in the world, she always came home to me with a sunny disposition that always soothed me. I snapped my fingers once, and her eyes cracked to mine.

"I missed you today, love. How was your day?" I asked, and her eyes lit up.

"I missed you more, honey. Today, Ta'iah told me that she would only be coming into the shop a few days a week, and that almost made me have an anxiety attack."

"Why didn't you call me? Come and sit, my llove, and tell me about your feelings."

I reached my hand toward her, and she obliged by taking hold. She stepped over the candles and bent over to kiss my lips succulently. Her kisses always breathed life into me. I indulged in the lusciousness of her lips for a few before she sat down and mirrored my sitting.

"Continue, my love."

"It wasn't nothing too serious, honey. I'm just not big on personal customer interactions. Ta'iah and I have waited so long for these opportunities to be with the men of our dreams, so I can stand in for her as she enjoys her happiness."

When she said that, my pride in her grew.

"My selfless little bird. You are so kind and considerate, and that makes me dig you so much more. That is why it excites me to offer you another level of intimacy tonight. In these situations, the stipulations I set forth are sometimes more than what un-evolved minds can comprehend.

I thank you for not only meeting me at the mind but being willing to sacrifice something as important as physical intimacy. You embrace my way of living like a fish to water. I value your strength and tenacity, and I'm glad that you are mine. I told you that my whole reason for breathing is to elevate your mind.

Tonight I will offer you a new way to achieve intimacy. Tonight is not a consolation prize but more of a different way to approach all that we are building. All I need you to do is follow my lead. Come sit in my lap with your legs on either side of me."

Anita moved to do as I described. The position we're sitting in is called Yab-Yum. This classic tantric sex position represents the union of Shiva and Shakti, the two divine energies of masculine and feminine. I placed my hands upon her waist and commanded her eyes with mine.

We stared in each other's eyes, silently communicating. In Anita's eyes, I saw redemption, hope, understanding, and admiration. Very soon, our breathing synchronized, and our heartbeats matched. The energy began to shift between us, so I lifted my hands from her waist and began to move the energy around her aura. I never broke eye contact as I drew her energy into mine and pushed them back into her combined.

Anita's eyes began to glaze a little, and her irregular breathing showed me my ministrations were hitting their intended target. My love was an earnest, attentive, and willing pupil. With her eyes under my rapt attention and our energy bubbling beneath her core, I began to softly recite the piece I'd worked on in her absence.

"Today, I sat here, just thinking lovely thoughts about you. As I ruminated, my mind began to drift. My mind went outside of the realm of reality, landing in a perfect fantasy staring us.

In this place, you greeted me with a gentle lover's kiss as I enveloped you in the secure, warm comfort of my arms. I tried to get so close that we combined into one person. We stood there, as I whispered sweet nothings, that strung together melodically in your ear like a love song. We were finally on one accord.

Before you knew it, we were prostrate together. I began kissing you from eyelid to toe-tip and then reversing. Reverently, I used my limbs to pay homage to your infinite femininity. Slowly, I indulged in all of the delicacies your womanhood had to offer. After immersing my senses completely, I stop, bringing myself to rest outside of your dwelling place.

We locked hands in spiritual agreement. We locked eyes in complete awareness of the other's spirit. As we were silently conversing with one another, you inhale, I am home. When you exhale, welcome me in, baby. Each movement becomes an expression of what we feel.

My utterings equate to pure love sentences. We feel it as the heat suffuses our systems. My strength is clenching in unison. We feel the heavens open up, and our hearts kiss, for we are breasts to chest. The floodgates open up, and we both let go."

Anita had tears leaking down her cheeks. I could feel the tremors subtly taking over her body. My feeling mirrored hers, and the erratic beats of her hearts were mine. My phallus was taut with desire, and I could feel the phantom clenching of her womb. Our skin dripped sweat due to the unspent energy, and it was only one thing to say to relieve our pressure before we combusted.

"Come with me, love!"

Our bodies followed my command. I erupted from the middle of my soul in endless ropes as Anita's river flowed and drowned us all. All the while, we never broke the connection in our peepers. It was the most beautifully erotic scene I've experienced in my life. When our bodies were spent, I pulled her close and whispered sweet nothings in her ear; Anita cried and praised my value in her life.

My soul felt bonded to her on a spiritual level, and I knew I would be adding this experience to our routine. I lifted us off the floor and walked us to our room. I sat Anita on her feet as I went into the bathroom and ran us a bath. Once done, I grabbed Anita and took her into the bathroom where we both cleaned our sins from one another's body.

After we finished, we dried one another and prepared for bed as usual. We cuddled and talked, and I prepared Anita for my absence. I had a business trip that would monopolize my time. Although I wouldn't be with her physically, I would continue to protect her with my life. Soon, Anita was snoring, and I followed behind her into dreamland, counting down the minutes until I could have her this way again.

Chapter 10: Anita

I swear for lawd, our clientele at *Purrrfect Kitty* lived to make me go bald around the edges. I was kind of overwhelmed because Ta'iah's and I schedules have been all over the place since we both met our men. She worked from his house more than she came in, so that left me to have to deal with these customers face-to-face.

"Ma'am, I'm trying to explain to you that you have to buy a strap-on with a harness proportioned to your size. I tried to tell you that I was only suggesting the leather because it is the sturdiest material we have," I explained, exasperatingly, to the woman that stood before me, giving me a major attitude regarding our products.

It was people like her that threw my anxiety through the roof and made my skin crawl. They tried to tell us that the customer was always right, but I say fuck that. Some of these customers needed to be thrown in trunks and hefted off a bridge.

"You don't have to use all those fancy words to try to shade me for being big-boned. Maybe you guys shouldn't use such cheap material to make these products, and I wouldn't have to keep coming back and wasting my money on these fraudulent items. You are getting on my nerves, ole smart-mouth heifer."

Her voice gave me an instant headache. The name-calling made all my southern hospitality leave me at that moment. I had time today to stoop to her level.

"Let me explain something, you big bi—"

I heard a snap, and my head raised. There stood Sterling. He clapped his hands three times, so I left my disgruntled customer where she was and found my way over to him. Sterling had moved to behind our handcuff display. I stood in front of him, awaiting direction.

"Love, finish with your customer, and do it with a smile. When you finish, lock the door and meet me in the back. Before you come, grab the leather paddle on the third row down off the wall. I expect you in under five minutes."

He kissed my forehead, then walked off and headed to the back.

His commands made me nervous, but I hurried to complete his tasks. I proceeded over to my customer, and after offering her the product she refused *for free*, she became very jolly. After telling me she didn't know what kind of freaky-deeky shit I was into, but she liked what it did to my attitude, I rang her up and bagged her items before hurrying her to the exit.

Once she was on the other side of my door, I locked it and thought about the task Sterling gave me. I could feel my attitude all over my body; she made me mad down to my toenails with her insufferable attitude. I proceeded to my wall which housed our display of paddles. Then, I grabbed the one which he had requested off the wall and stomped my way towards the back.

When I arrived at the back of the store where we usually held our presentations, I saw Sterling, and he did not look pleased. I had never really experienced the look on his face nor that posture, but it looked fierce. I stepped into the room, and it felt heavy.I didn't understand the tension.

It had been weeks since I'd gone home with him, and the only way I can describe it was pure bliss. We had a routine that was full of spontaneity and adventure. I had only been rewarded for what I offered him daily. As I stared at him, it seemed as if a reward was the furthest thing from his mind, and that didn't fit the normal for us.

I made it to the middle of the room and stood there. Sterling's severe aura let me know that it wasn't wise to proceed a step closer and try to embrace him lovingly. Which was something I did every time I was in his presence, as a way of greeting or pure affection. To watch him as he stood there with a stern gaze but a disappointed look on his face, made me tremble with uncertainty.

Sterling was leaning against the wall with his arms folded. I didn't know what to feel about his look or his stance. For endless minutes, Sterling stared at me intensely, and it made me feel as bare as a naked hitchhiker on a highway soliciting a ride. That was just how severe and unnerving his look made me feel.

I held the paddle in front of me as if it covered me from his scrutiny. Sterling removed himself from the wall and walked until he stood a foot in front of me. All you could hear was his irregular angered breathing as he watched me for a few moments before he started speaking.

"Anita, do you care to explain to me why I came into your workplace, to surprise you, nontheless, and witness you acting a fool? All I thought about was getting here to you after my business trip kept me from home for a few days. Explain to me why the first visuals of my love, are you acting way less than ladylike? Especially to someone that patronizes your business!" He asked me, and I felt ashamed that he witnessed my interaction with the village idiot.

"Honey—"

"You will call me, *Sir*."

I gulped audibly and felt my eyes water a little bit. I had never addressed him with anything but loving words. To call him, *Sir*, felt awkward, but I wasn't in control.

"Sir...I had been dealing with very difficult customers all day. This particular customer had been antagonizing me. It made me upset, and I felt at my wit's end." I offered him the best explanation I could think of for what he witnessed.

"So, because you had been dealing with the pressures of the day, it made you act in a manner unbefitting a woman? You were going to call your customer out her name and possibly use more than a few choice of vulgarities because you were frustrated."

"But she was—"

"*Shut your mouth!*" He yelled before he stepped into my personal bubble.

I was trembling even harder now because he had never raised his voice at me before. I dropped my head because I knew that he was disappointed in me, and I couldn't face him.

"Eyes up!! Do not bow your head again. Do you understand?"

I picked up my head and nodded it in affirmation of his command. Sterling plucked me in my collarbone. The sting reminded me that I needed to answer him with my words.

"Yes, Sir, I understand."

When I answered him, Sterling began to pace back in forth. Not in an angry trot or anything of that nature, but more of a languid back and forth. The motions set your nerves on the edge of what was to come.

"My Anita, I'm so disappointed in you. I have told you time and again that I am responsible for you. Every responsibility that I have, I take seriously. You are a direct reflection of me. From your mannerisms to your actions, you have to show the perfect guidance of my leadership. Do you feel as if you reflected me at my best? By your attitude, does it show that you have a good leader? One who takes his time and energy molding you into a supreme being."

"No, Sir," I respond lowly

"What is the character of a woman?" He asked me.

"A woman is humble and willing to be taught. She gives all of what she has selflessly. She smiles in the face of adversity and handles all situations with grace and poise. Even if the world seems to be crumbling, she must appear cool, calm, and collected. A woman does not use vulgar words, ugly speech, or unkind epithets. The reason being, her beauty should be felt in everything she exudes, especially her speech."

"*Exactly.* Every situation is an opportunity for others to either be amazed by or become disgusted with your character. I hate to say it, but I'm feeling the latter. I watched you unnoticed for over an hour. You seemed wound up an unapproachable. You were offering half-smiles and even lesser customer service. I watched you treat other humans as if they were beneath you, and that makes me angry. The only question I have is, what made you act in that manner? Think before you speak."

Sterling kept his eyes intently on me as I racked my brain, trying to take a close introspection of my actions. I had been feeling entirely off all morning. It was like today wasn't my day. From the moment I opened my eyes, I was upset and couldn't temper the emotion no matter how hard I tried.

I started pondering about if anything happened new or out of the norm. The only thing I could think of was… Aha! I had a moment of clarity. Sterling had not been home for three days, nor had I spoken to him for two of those days. Vividly, I remembered feeling sad and neglected at first, but on the third day, I was mad as hell. I didn't know those feelings would manifest anywhere except the inside of my soul, where I felt I had suppressed them.

"Sir, I have been missing you, and the loneliness became too much. I felt several different emotions, but today, anger was most prominent." I revealed my truth to him and unburdened my heart.

"Love, I understand that my absence may have thrown you through a loop, but I'm never too far away from you. I watched you on the in-home cameras to make sure you were safe. I tried to teach you that absence makes the heart grow fonder. I wanted you to take the yearning you had for me and wrap it in a welcome that would have blown my mind. Except, I came home to a sight that was not the likes."

Sterling's words made me feel thoroughly reprimanded. In hindsight, I accept that I acted a little prematurely. Now, my ill-temperament and uncouth mannerisms might have cost me my spot. No Dominant wanted someone unteachable, or one who couldn't think outside of her own needs. The thought of him severing ties caused my panic to rise.

"Sir, I'm so sorry about the selfishness of my actions. I promise that I take your teachings very seriously.

Please don't give up on me. I promise I will do better. I do apologize for causing you such disappointment."

I was openly crying. Surprisingly,Sterling came to hug me and wipe my tears.

"Shhh...love, stop crying. You are doing exceptional, and until today, I have not been disappointed in you. I realize that you do need further teaching. Nonetheless, you are a great student, so I expect these next lessons to drive home my point. I accept your apology and the sincerity in which you gave it. Still, unfortunately, you must pay for your unbecoming behavior. Hand me the paddle," Sterling demanded with his hand out.

I gave him the paddle, and he pointed two fingers straight down to the floor. I automatically bent over and touched my toes. I felt him move behind me before he lifted my dress, resting the bottom on my lower back. Sterling pulled my boy shorts down until they caught around my thighs.

"Today, you have shown your ass. You've embarrassed me and made a mockery of your training, and most of all, shamed yourself. I never wanted to use corporal punishment to correct your errant behavior, but I must so that you may understand. Understand that in my presence, or my absence, I expect excellence, and there will be no excuses for anything less. Will you accept this punishment?"

"Yes, Sir, I accept," I responded with no hesitation.

"Keep your hands locked on your ankles. Do not make a sound. Do not move. Disobey any directive, and we will begin again. I will tan your hide until I'm certain you understand."

Tan my hide he did. I stopped counting after fifteen lashes. When he finished meting out punishment, he pulled my underwear back up and placed my dress back down. Afterward, Sterling took me home to nurse my wounds. I went to bed that night with a lesson learned and a willingness to learn all that I could.

Chapter 11: Sterling

I had been punishing Anita for the better part of a week. One punishment being, taking away her morning satisfaction. Morning satisfaction was a routine part of our day that set the tone for prosperity in our household. Our routine involved me diving headfirst into her ocean and getting my chin wet. It was scientifically proven that orgasms in the morning relaxed your mind and nerves during the day. The endorphins released went a long way toward ensuring happiness.

I have been showing her how to exercise patience. There was no better way to teach her that, than pushing her body to limits to enforce self-control. I had been taking her to the edges of orgasms and then never allowing her to finish. On the precipice, Anita would hang, and there was not a thing she could do to take herself over the edge. The act was beauty in suspension. At least, that's how I would describe those moments of her sexual helplessness.

There have been times when she had been on the brink of tears, but I didn't fold nor let her cum. I stood firm in my lessons so that we would never have to go through this torture again. Anita would never know how her punishment was felt on my end because I derived pleasure from pleasing her. So, in essence, denying Anita has been me denying myself.

What has made her feel chastised was that I would not allow her to touch me. I may be a little Asexual, but I did enjoy the occasional hand job, blow job, or mutual masturbation. We have not even engaged in Tantra, which is the exchange of energy interspersed with your sexual activities. Tantra was something that we did three times a week, and I had taken that off the menu as well.

Some days, I had even restrained her while I played with a butterfly vibrator at different speeds until she was writhing in pain from holding in her desire. No matter what I've done to frustrate Anita, she has taken the challenge with grace. She still gets up in the morning to make my breakfast and does so with a smile. I have popped in on her at work, and she is chipper and more amenable. That's commendable even with some of the pills she has to swallow in her day.

I have been shocked by her transformation, and it made me proud to see how she'd applied my corrections.

I was sitting in my office at the community center, preparing for a meeting. It was a meeting with the young lady who won the showcase and her parents. Her mother and father were not in attendance the day she presented. Only her paternal grandmom had attended, and she didn't want to be responsible for the check. Her grandmom also wanted the parents to get a DVD of their daughter presenting, and we were happy to oblige.

In the middle of me doing paperwork, there was a knock on the door. Hastily, I sat up and put the papers away before I announced that they could enter. When the family walked through the door, I was smiling brightly. That's until my eyes went past the little girl and her father and landed on her mother. I would know that face anywhere. It was like mine except more feminine and beautiful.

The same birthmark and eyes are upon a more mature face. I can't believe that before me was my sister, Shelisa, and I became overcome with emotion. Then, I heard a throat clear.

"Umm, hello, bossman, you know my wife?"

I heard the aggression in his voice. That made me turn to look at him.He appeared to be a bit thuggish, but I could care less. I was raised in the heart of North Philly, and my heart feared no man.

"I know Lee-Lee better than you think." I couldn't help but fuck with him.

"Yo', you got me fucked up talking 'bout you know my wife better—"

"Bae, calm down, and *you* cut it out. He does know me better than you because he is my brother. My God, Sterly, I can't believe that it's you."

She rushed around the desk,fell in my arms, and began crying. I held onto my sister tightly, trying to make up for the many years worth of hugs we missed.

We were separated as children. It had been more than twenty years since I had laid eyes on my first baby. Shelisa is almost five years younger than me, and we were as close as any two siblings could be.

"I'm happy for this family reunion and all, but we came to talk about this little lady right here," my new brother-in-law said to me.

I almost forgot why we were even in my office. It felt good to hold someone with the same blood flowing through their veins as me. Honestly, I have missed that feeling of familial ties.

"You are correct, and I'm sorry for yanking your chain earlier. I just couldn't help myself. I was just so happy to see my sister after all this time. You just don't know what I'm feeling right now. My name is Sterling, by the way." I told him honestly.

He reached his hand out to me, and I gave him a handshake.

"I can respect that. I just don't play about my wife. Shelisa is the greatest thing that ever happened to me, and I have no problem going to war behind, or for her. The name is Solid, Solid Bridges," he responds in kindness, and I love that my sister had a protector.

"That's all love right there. Well, I'm sure you all have heard about the fantastic job Genuine did in her presentation. Her idea was not only innovative, but it's way ahead of her time. She wowed not only me, but the judges as well. Genuine not only earned a check to support all that she needs to develop such a great application. She has also earned a ten-week internship with myself to help her learn about marketing tools, and I will also coordinate meetings with investors. She is one of the brightest minds that we have attending the programs here. You should both be very proud."

"That's what I'm talking about, right there. My baby is a little prodigy. I told you she was beyond her years when she came out looking around the room like she had questions for the world," Solid happily responded.

"Oh, my word, this is so amazing. This opportunity more than humbles her father and me. We have been working to make sure our baby had better experiences than we did growing up," my sister said.

"Well, this is the way you begin. You give them better lives by exposing their minds to different things. You stand behind all their dreams until they become a reality. I can tell that she is well adjusted at home, and every instructor we have sings her praises. Genuine is a reflection of dedicated parenting, and it shows in everything that she does."

We spent a few more moments discussing my new niece and filling out the necessary forms for the internship before I handed them the check. I exchanged numbers with both of them and set up the dates and times for her internship. Time just seemed to slip by before they made their excuses for a departure, and we all said goodbye to one another.

When they left, I had time to think about the separation of my sister and myself. It wasn't something that either one of us could control. It saddened me that instead of growing up together, one adult's corrupt desires ripped us apart.

I think of all the firsts I missed with Shelisa. Things like her going to the prom or on her first date. The opportunity to scare off all the nappy-headed boys that started to show an interest in her. The right to walk her down the aisle and giving her advice about life.

I think of the nights that I cried tears deep from the middle of my soul from missing her. Wishing that she could just bust in my room and annoy me one more time, or she would demand I entertain her with my created stories. The innocence of playing tea party with her at her demand because she wasn't gon' just talk to stuffed animals.

It all caused me to laugh at the memories of a time when I was happy, but also, a time where I felt unsafe. A time where Shelisa never understood how being close to her was a way for me to protect her silently. All that I sacrificed to ensure that she would not become a statistic. How my shadows placed me in a perpetual state of fear, but her light soothed me. I needed her as much as she needed me.

It had been years since I have delved into those dark places that disrupted my spirit. I had been great at creating a perfect reality—a reality where nothing before our separation ever existed. Seeing my sister again made me remember that I was, by birthright, a Carter. A legacy far removed from myself, but one I wore as a reminder of all that I lost and overcame at the same time.

That impromptu reunion began to make me feel anxious. My world seemed knocked off its axis. If only I could remember to breathe. *Come on, Sterling, you are more than your memories.* I was trying to talk myself down from a full meltdown. Shelisa's presence, although comforting, had also caused an unexpected domino effect.

I began to see flashes of long ago buried scenes. The questions and uncertainties within myself were trying to be set free. I knew what I needed, and that was to be reminded that I was strong. Affirmation that I was still in control of my existence. The wise folks once said, "This too shall pass," but it felt like the pain would never stop. I began to search for my phone, frantically.

I shot my love a text with precise instructions. Then, I packed up and left my office. I had to get to my point of safety so that this could all go away. Once I got home, I could become the master of my destiny again. Nothing or no one would be able to penetrate my fortress, and that alleviated some of my fears. I just had to get where my mind could be free, and no ghosts from my past could reach me.

I was finally home from work, and I was glad for the opportunity to take a load off. After removing my shoes at the door, I headed into my bedroom to change into something more comfortable. My body felt tired. It bordered on broken because for days on end, my punishment from sterling had dragged on.

Sterling had rigorously taken my body through the paces. Everything imaginable, from feathers to ice, from candle wax to handcuffs, and much more in-between. I had been through levels of being pushed to my limits without the reward of release. I missed the pleasure he provided me, but I understood that pleasure was a privilege and not obligatory.

Before the faux pas with my attitude, we had built a more than comfortable life together. One where we shared intimacy and companionship minus the sex. Well, not all sex, just penetration. The intimacy through touch and affection was more than enough to make our life one of normalcy even if it wasn't understood through society's standard of living.

The relationship that Sterling and I shared worked for us and needed no validation from outsiders. That was until "the punishment." Since then, Sterling no longer greeted me with kisses and kind words. There were no more shared meals and conversations at the end of a long day. The mornings where he used to jump-start my day orally, were long gone. I had not touched him, exchanged energy, or just sat in his presence while allowing his aura to soothe me in a week, and I felt saddened.

All I ever wanted to do was make him happy and be the reason for the admiration in his eyes. To know that I brought this all on myself was indeed the true punishment. Sterling, in a short time, had become essential to my every day functioning in life. To feel how he had pulled back, turned me into an overachiever.

All of his lessons have damn near broken me, but it approached my punishment with a different kind of thinking. Now, when he was teaching me, I immediately applied those lessons to other facets of life. For hours every night, he took my body and mind through changes. It was all in hopes of teaching me patience. At least, that was what I believed was the goal for all of his many lessons.

Each day I woke up in the morning, I took care of him as I had always done. It would start with breakfast and his favorite reading material with classical music in the mornings. I would then head to work where those nightly sessions finally made sense.

Customer Service had never been my strong suit. I had been shy around and wary of humans my whole life. You factor in their bad attitudes and demanding ways, and for me, it was a recipe for disaster. Because although I have been shy, I also have a very volatile reactionary attitude. But I have learned to temper my attitude through Sterling and his wise ways. I've learned that you can't control the people in your atmosphere, but you could control how much of your energy you lent them to help create chaos in your world.

Every day, I saw that my kindness went a long way in killing unkind attitudes. Finally, I realized that everything did not deserve a reaction, and people were not prone to argue with themselves or positive vibes. It took for this amazing man to take away my comfortability to drive home that point. A point that I should conduct myself above board, as well as treat others with the same thoughtfulness and respect I desired from him. It had been a hard but necessary lesson.

I was just lying across the bed in deep thought when my phone pinged with a message. I grabbed it to see who was contacting me this time of the night. When I saw the name, I smiled real big.

Honey: Love, you have shown me that you are worth my forgiveness. You have taken everything I showed you and put it into practice. I'm proud of you, and tonight, your punishment will end. This night, I will give you back one of the many comforts I've deprived you. Tonight, I will allow you to be reminded of the human touch. Your hands may have forgotten the knowledge of me, but they will remember once again. You can reintroduce me to all that you are while I bask in your energy. Let's commune together through mind, body, and sensuality. I am the canvass, and you are the artist. Paint this perfect picture of us.

I jumped up excitedly because this was just the moment I had been waiting to receive. I was looking for a way to redeem myself. The punishment was over, and I intended to celebrate its end. I had the perfect idea of exactly what I was going to do.

I grabbed a pen and paper to leave Sterling a note and then ran around to set the mood. I had a fire lit under my ass, and I was going to make our night perfect. After making sure the candles were lit and the rose petals were spread around, I grabbed all the materials I would need to make our night one to remember.

Once everything was all set up and ready to go, I went into my room to get my hygiene together. I used my brown sugar, honey, and ginseng body scrub to cleanse my skin and invigorate my energy. I was trying to embody a state of calm. I had to get my mind right to enjoy this gift that I would receive.

Once inside my room, I began to rummage through my closet for clothes. I picked out the perfect outfit, then went to lay it upon my bed before taking a seat in the middle of the bed. With my mind focused, I sat Indian style and began to meditate.

Meditation was something that Sterling introduced to me, and I thoroughly enjoyed it now. It was all about getting your mind and body in sync. Centering my energy, I slowly felt my limbs relax, and my breathing become even.

Once I feel my mind and body sync, I opened my eyes and started getting ready. Tonight, I had chosen a Traditional Japanese Yukata in black with blue, white, and red cherry blossoms. It was made of linen, so it flowed against my skin. Then, I grabbed the Black Tabi Socks and placed them on my feet. When I finished, I stood in the mirror to tie the red sash around my Yukata.

Picking up my wire hairbrush, I began to brush my hair back into a bun. Once I tamed my mane, I searched my accessory chest for a pair of red chopsticks and applied them to the bun. I decided to leave my face makeup-free outside of the red lip-glass I applied to my lips. Hurriedly, I head downstairs into the room that I'd chosen for the scene of our reconnection.

As I stood there in the room with the ambiance set, I became a ball of nerves. I had never taken the initiative to go this hard to impress Sterling with all that he'd taught me. But since he placed a monumental task on my shoulders, I was aiming to please more than his body. Nobody knew the trepidation I felt. Planning an occasion to wow someone whose mind was a thing of beauty, and who to date, had created all of our moments.

Sterling entrusting my mind was a reward all in itself. He was a natural-born leader, so him giving me a modicum of control when in these situations, there was only dictation, was overwhelming. It gave me the push I needed to rise to the occasion and view the moment as a test that I refused to fail.

Foot-to-foot I bounced just awaiting and trying to release the last jitters I felt. I heard the front door opening and the alarm disarming. With that sound, I immediately calmed. I held my position and waited for Sterling to find me. By that time, he should have gotten the note and nightcap I left for him.

All he had to do was follow the trail of roses I laid out, leading to the room. I wanted to show him that royalty he deserved to have the crème of nature laid at his feet. No matter how nervous I was on the inside, I was cool as a cucumber on the outside. For seconds upon minutes, I waited until I heard the knob turn on the door that would lead him to me.

Sterling walked in the door, and my pussy began beatboxing. He stood before me with his shirt unbuttoned, and his tie was hanging loosely. Sterling then took a moment to survey the room and all that I had prepared for him. He smiled brightly before he snapped his fingers twice, and I proceeded to him expeditiously.

When I was within arms reach, he pulled me into a tight, loving embrace. Sterling grabbed my face in his hands, placed his lips upon mine, and pecked me three times. Then, he kissed my eyelids and, eventually, my forehead. The reverence in his touch made me cry tears of joy. I missed his affection.

Sterling pulled me close. As he inhaled my scent, I felt my energy flow into him, and when he finally exhaled, I received his in return.

"My love, you have pleased me beyond my wildest dreams. I'm almost afraid to see what else you have in store for me. It satisfies my mind to see you pull off this endeavor. I trusted in your ability to take direction, and you exceeded my expectations. From my favorite drink to the best of God's nature that I walked upon, then to this relaxing mood. Now let's see what else you have in store."

I pulled back out of his embrace and started undressing him. When he was in all his naked glory, I walked him over to the massage table. I gestured for him to lay on the table. Once he laid down, I placed a sheet over his waistline that fell to the back of his thighs.

Walking over to the oil warmer, I selected the unique oil mixture of ylang-ylang, ginger, ginseng, and cinnamon. The mixture would be vital to give the massage the maximum effect since I wanted to give Sterling an extraordinary experience. I placed a nice sized dollop in my hand and began working his muscles. Starting at his feet and working my way up his body. My hands were trembling a little because I had not felt his skin underneath my hands in so long. It felt incredible, and I relished in the feeling.

By the time I began working on his back, Sterling's muscles were fully relaxed. I felt every piece of tension leave his body as I molded his muscles like a potter. When I got to his shoulders, his arm dropped off the table. Sterling began to run his hands up my leg languidly. When he got to my waist, he squeezed tightly and then pulled me close to his face. Sterling sniffed my kitty, and the debauchery of his action caused my flesh to break out in goosebumps. He untied the sash in the back, and my Yukata fell open.

Sterling pulled me closer as he turned his head and body around on the table. I was standing there looking down on him with my hands frozen in place. He nosed my vagina, and I was slightly embarrassed because she had been leaking since I touched him. Sterling was giving my clit Eskimo-kisses; that made me leak more profusely. Pulling back, Sterling stuck two fingers straight up in the air, and I immediately raised my hands.

"Take three steps back and do not drop your hands."

Instantly, I do as he requested. Sterling came off the table, and he dropped to his knees in front of me. He snatched my hips and pulled me close to his face.

"I haven't been full since the last time I tasted you. Your aroma is the most inviting, and your taste is like no other," he said to my pussy, and then French kissed her.

I could feel my knees buckling, but he had such a firm hold on my waist that it prevented me from folding. The pleasure almost made me drop my hands, but my fear of missing out on this delicious treat kept my hands juxtaposed in the air. Every lick, suck and kiss were felt past my womb into my being. The heat was gathering in my soul and spreading out. I felt like I was about to combust.

"Permission to cum, honey?"

"Permission denied. Lay on the table, hands up, legs spread, and mouth open, now!" He demands, and I flew to the table, assuming the position.

Once I was laid down, mouth wide as the Sahara with my eyes on him, Sterling came swaggering over to the table. He began caressing my hair and face touching my lips like they were a delicacy.

"I need you to eat this dick up like you are starving, then let me paint your face."

As soon as he starts feeding me his dick, I inhale it like I missed a month worth of meals. His flavor was unique, and I was thirsty for it. As soon as he hits the back of my throat, I loosen it, then tighten it while swirling my tongue. It had the desired effect.

"Yes...fuck, make that shit nasty...just like that. Ahhh, fuck!"

He began to fuck the lining out of my throat, and I didn't break a sweat. When he started going crazy, I began gurgling in the back of my throat. That was all she wrote. Sterling snatched his dick out of my mouth and created a masterpiece all over my face.

"Head upstairs and into my room. There is no work for you tomorrow."

With a face full of cum, I headed upstairs into his room. I was so ready for this night and all that he had in store for me. I put my game face on and prepared for my next lesson.

Chapter 13: Sterling

I was headed over to my sister's house. Ever since the day we reconnected at the center, we had been in very close contact. We spoke almost every day, and it was good to have a sense of family again. I had even introduced Shelisa to Anita, and they hit it off like two old friends. I never had to explain my relationship with Anita because Anita played her position so well that no questions ever arose.

Shelisa and I would video chat daily to catch up on life and what's changed throughout the years. We never went too deep because I just wanted her to know the man I had become. It was not necessary to remember the boy I once was.

I pulled up to her house, which was in North Philly. I offered to move her closer to me, to which she took offense. She didn't feel comfortable anywhere else, and I respected her position. As long as she felt safe, that was all I cared to know.

I locked up my car and headed up the steps to her front door. It was crazy because we used to live two blocks up the street from where Shelisa now resided. I haven't seen some of these sights in over two decades.

Her front door opened, and there stood my brother-in-law. He was beginning to look a little better from the last time I saw him about three weeks ago. At that time, he was banged up pretty bad. Now, he appeared to be moving exponentially better as he opened the screen door.

"Hey, bro, how you?" Solid said while reaching his hand out and I grasped it in a firm handshake

"I'm good, homie. Just came to pick my niece up for our weekly bonding time," I said while walking into the house.

"That's what's up. Genuine has been up for hours getting prepared for this day. It's all she talks about from the time you drop her off on Sunday until you pick her up the following Saturday," he said to me while we took a seat on the couch.

"I love to hear that Genuine loves hanging out with her favorite uncle. But in other news, how are you holding up? You seem to be getting around better."

"Man, I am doing way better. I just feel bad knowing that I almost lost my life. That is enough for me not to mind the limping nor the aches and pains."

Solid said that as if he was deep in thought or reliving the tragedy.

"Do you mind telling me what happened? I mean, if I'm not prying or anything," I asked him, trying to get him out of his deep thoughts.

"Let's just say that my decisions almost cost me my life, but I'm grateful that my presence was felt, and I was given a second chance. I wanted to ask you something."

"Sure, go ahead. Shoot."

"Your sister has been my rider from the bottom, and no matter how hard I have gone in these streets, she has rocked with me. Shelisa has never made me feel less than a man, nor has she not supported any decision I made for this family. When she gave me Genuine, I knew I was going to have to go a little harder to get out of my line of work quicker.

But I found myself in a jam and will be leaving soon to go to training camp as a condition to get out of this jam. What I want to know is if you can watch over my family until this is done? I know she doesn't want to leave the hood, but I need to know my daughter and wife are safe while I'm away from home."

"Of course, that is without question. My family is safe wherever I am."

Solid breathed a sigh of relief at my statement.

"Good, man. Thanks for that. That leads me to another thing. They will have to leave with you today since I have to report at the post tonight."

"That is no problem. Let me get some things arranged, and as long as they are packed, we can go now," I let him know

"Alright, man. I really appreciate this. Let me go up here and see what's taking my family so long."

While he went to check on them, I pulled my phone out to shoot Anita a text.

Me: Hey, love. Would you mind getting the guest house together for my sister and niece who will be staying for awhile?

My Love: No problem, dear. I will do this now. Will that be all you need?

Me: Yes, I am going to head over to the market with them and grab a few extra things. Please send me a list.

My Love: Will do, I will have the list ready momentarily.

Me: Thank you, sweetness. I shall see you soon

"Uncle! I am so happy you are here."

I turn to see my niece running towards me. I scooped her up in my arms and hugged her close. I looked over Genuine's head, and my sister was standing there with puffy eyes that are red from crying. Shelisa's husband had her wrapped up in his arms, whispering to her. He was consoling her, and she seemed inconsolable. I sat my niece down on her feet.

"Aww, Lee-Lee, am I chopped liver? You are acting like he's sending you to a dungeon. Crying all hard like he sending you to walk the plank."

My sister burst out laughing at that and came to hug me. It felt good to be able to comfort her. At least she still needed her big brother.

"No, I am happy to spend time with you. I have just never been apart from my husband for an extended amount of time in the whole nine years we have been together. Until you came back in my life, he and Genuine were the only family I had. But I'm okay in your care. Bae, let's start taking the bags to the car."

My brother-in-law and I started taking the bags to the car. Once my niece was secured, I hopped in the driver's seat. Solid and my sister were standing outside of the car, talking for a minute. She placed her hand upon his face, and then he kissed her so passionately and deeply. I ended up turning my head as not to intrude on such an intimate private moment.

My sister jumped into the car, and she is no longer crying nor sad. It seemed that her attitude had taken a complete one-eighty. She now sat in the front seat, bubbling with excitement.

"Did you let Anita know we were coming? I don't want to impose, especially with your relationship being so new. I just wanted to make sure you have permission to have guests," Shelisa asked me.

"Of course, although it wasn't necessary. I ask for permission from no one. Whatever I say is law in my house. But I understand where you are coming from. I mentioned it to her, so chill. I do have manners."

"Don't be an ass. It doesn't suit you. You just better have some manners. I understand it's your house, but if she resides there, you have to consider her feelings. She is the queen of your castle."

"How many times do I have to tell you that Anita and I are not in a conventional relationship? We are two people who love each other's energy, time, and space. Nothing more, nothing less, and you are making it bigger than it is. I'm certain she doesn't place these types of emphasis on the situation as you do. Silly girl with a rich imagination."

"Umm-hmm, no matter how you slice or dice it, if you open up your home to a woman, then it means more. I see the way you look at her and the way she caters to you. Being around you both is electric and makes the mind inquire. It's almost borderline kinky. But anyway, you can try to downplay it if you want to, but she is gon' be my sister-in-law. You mark my words."

I didn't even try to explain it to her any further. Clearly, the little lady had made it up in her mind that I would be willing to give her a traditional relationship to rejoice about. You couldn't explain to people the dynamics of the perfection of what Anita and I shared. It went beyond a traditional relationship. Our vibe was more than Domination and Submission. Anita had allowed me to take her mind to new heights and has shown me that being led is more than a desire for her.

We pulled up to Fresh Grocer and exited the car. My niece was bouncing with the excitement that only children got when going to the grocery store. I was caught up in the innocence in which she viewed the building full of endless possibilities. We grabbed a cart, but Genuine was too big to ride inside of it, so I allow her to stand on the back to help me guide the cart.

"Lee-Lee, I want you to pick out somethings that you and my niece generally eat. I want you both to be comfortable, so spare no expense."

That seemed to be all I needed to say. I watched my sister grab herself a cart, so I knew we were about to rack up on some good food.

I pulled out my phone to see what Anita had put on our list. It didn't seem that long of a list, so I memorized it and then put my phone away. We started our shopping excursion in the fruit and vegetable aisle. My niece's eyes light up, and Genuine tickled me with her animated expressions. Most children today didn't value fresh fruits and vegetables because their parents didn't buy them. I helped Genuine pick out kiwis, bananas, starfruit, and pineapples. Along with kale, spinach, and broccoli. We shopped while Genuine told me about all the things that happened in her young world.

I grabbed the strawberries, blueberries, and grapes that Anita loved to eat in the mornings. It seemed as if I always mindlessly thought of the smallest things to please her. How could I not when Anita was so good to me? My niece was just grabbing things, and like the typical uncle with no kids of his own, I indulged all of her whims and desires.

We turned down the cereal aisle as I was trying to find this flaxseed and granola cereal that I loved for breakfast. The market always seemed to be sold out when I came looking for it. I found the cereal on the bottom shelf, so I bent over to retrieve a few boxes in order to stock the pantry.

"That ass still looks as sweet as I remember. Such a shame it's all grown up. Nothing like when it was young and willing."

When I heard those words, I became frozen in place. It couldn't be him in the middle of a random crowded market. I felt my body begin to perspire, and I was trembling a little bit. Automatically, I stood to my feet, but I couldn't turn around. I felt like that lost little boy from long ago. Maybe if I closed my eyes, he and what he represented would disappear.

I was on an island enjoying the sights and sounds of nature. Nothing was around me except for the waves singing their song as they lapped against the shore. I was all alone being one with the elements. Most of all, I was safe. I tried to convince my mind to stay put until I felt my vision invaded with the warmth at my ear.

"You still the same little bitch you have always been. You cut off all that pretty hair, but you're still as delicious as ever. Look how afraid you are when you know I love the fear. I bet I could still slide in between those cheeks and make you cum.

I still remember those pretty young lips wrapped around my dick. I trained you so well. I bet you never felt the inside of a woman for craving this hard dick. You want me to take it, you little bitch. I know you miss it."

Then, I felt his hands attempting to grope my dick. That's when I lost my entire mind. I snatched out of his grasp and finally turned around with fire in my eyes. There stood my greatest nightmare.

He looked the same at 6'3, muscle-bound, and manly on the outside. In his eyes was the same perverted look of a man that ruined childhoods and shattered dreams. He was standing there, smirking at me with a sick and lascivious look. My uncle, my flesh and blood, was standing in a crowded grocery store acting worse than a stranger on the prowl for a kidnapping victim. He seemed to be waiting for a response from me.

A response was precisely what he got in the form of my Muay-Thai training. I gave him a high knee to the chest, followed by a quick jab and elbow combination. I commenced to whooping his ass up and down the cereal aisle. There was no letting up until I heard someone screaming in the distance, but still, it didn't deter me. I didn't know how many hand-feet, knee-elbow combinations I gave him. All I knew was I refused to stop.

"Sterling, please stop. We have your niece with us. Don't go to jail. He is not worth it."

My sister was imploring me, and her pleas were borderline desperate, so it snapped me out of my trance. I walked over my uncle like the trash that he was and kept it moving. I saw many of the patrons in the store clutching their pearls and shit. On any other day, I might've had a few fucks to give. But on this day, I am all out of fucks to give.

In the parking lot, I headed to my car, and all I could think about was leaving that dumbass place and getting to where I felt safe. I was shaking uncontrollably as I tried to unlock my car door. My keys kept dropping, and I couldn't get my bearings together to save my life. Frustrated, I laid my head on the side of my truck and tried to use the many breathing techniques I'd learned to calm my spirit. My anxiety was through the roof. I felt a touch on my lower back, and it caused me to jump out of my skin.

"Sterly, it is only me. Are you okay?"

Shelisa stood next to me with her arms raised in the air. I could tell she took a few steps back to give me space.

There were no words I could formulate to respond to her simple question. I just shook my head no, then opened the door and got inside. I waited for my family to get in the car and secure themselves before I sped out of the parking lot. The desperate need to get home was riding me hard. That was all I could focus on at that period of time.

"I knew you are feeling out of sorts. I understand why you just damn near killed our uncle, but you have to calm down. He didn't win brother. Please talk to me."

I wasn't trying to hear shit Shelisa had to say. I needed to get to my safe space and become normal again. Seeing my uncle after two decades was not what I needed in my life. Nor his presence. I turned the music on and blasted some tunes, not wanting to deal with idle chatter when a war was brewing inside of my soul.

He is a liar, liar, liar. I am a man.

I just kept repeating these things.

When we pulled up, I jumped out of the car and did a mad dash inside my home. *Safe place, where are you?*

I found her in the kitchen. Without preamble, I snatched her out of the chair and took off running to my bedroom. Once I was inside the room, I turn to her around and just stared at her. Anita seemed to be a little frazzled because I knew I looked bewildered.

"Honey, is everything okay?" she asked me with concern in her speech.

I didn't need words at that time. I needed validation. There was a burning desire to prove that my nightmare was lying. I pulled Anita to me and kissed her lips. The kiss was rougher than usual because I was trying to suck her life force out of her body. As I pulled back, my eyes roamed her from head to toe. Anita was wearing a dress that hugged her curves deliciously. Her breasts sat high but were firm and supple. Her hips flared out into an ass that appeared fuckable. That was what I was going to do.

I ripped the dress right down the middle. Anita had nothing on underneath, and it made my dick get as hard as calculus. Roughly, I pushed her onto the bed and proceeded to take my clothes off. Once I was naked, I laid my body parallel on top of Anita. I had to be inside of her before I succumbed to my own heart. This act was the defining moment for me. My manhood rested on the magnitude of that one act.

I didn't bother with foreplay as I was singularly focused. With my hands on my dick at Anita's entrance, I began to inch inside of her. Even without foreplay, she was wet and ready for me. I was meeting all types of resistance as I pushed inside of Anita. Knowing my size, I heard it could be overwhelming for some women during sex.

My intuition told me that I needed to just put it all inside of her before I changed my mind. On a hard thrust, I feel myself break through a barrier. If I had been in my right frame of mind at that moment, I would have realized that I just deflowered her. Well, I should say I just deflowered us because this was my first time ever laying inside of a woman's walls. The feeling I had lying inside of Anita's heaven was all the confirmation I needed.

"I am not gay. I am all, man."

With every stroke, I repeated that mantra. My hips began to move, and I closed my eyes. I thought about how many years I deprived myself of the perfect feeling that surrounded my dick. I felt myself getting lost in the excellence a pedophile tried to deter me from feeling. To finally have the bounty that God created for men overwhelmed my understanding. Anita's moans broke my reverie.

When I finally checked back into reality, I watched Anita caught in the throes of passion. No look had ever been as perfect as the one that blessed her face as I stroked her body. Vigorously, I grinded into her being willing her to confirm for me that I was all man. Anita was calling my name but begging God in the same breath. Her expressiveness inflated my ego to Mount Uhud proportions. Quickly, a tingling sensation started in my toes and rushed upwards. It happened so quickly, and before I knew it, I was burying my seeds deep in her womb.

My balls were empty, but my dick did not deflate, so I started the rhythm once again. At this moment, I just relished in the knowledge that my nightmares were finally being chased away. Inside of her, I don't feel less than a man. For once in my life, I'd felt whole. For the rest of the night, I enjoyed the new understanding Anita's womb gave me. I didn't know what the dawning of a new day would be, but for that time, I wanted to feel like a complete man. Nothing would stop me from chasing that feeling.

Where it led…

Chapter 14: Anita

My Love,

As I sit here watching you peacefully sleep after what we shared last night, I've come to many conclusions. One, I am selfish. I had no clue you were a virgin. I basically took and re-took your gift like a savage animal, and for that, I am sorry. Two, the strength I worked diligently to display has been compromised, and my judgment is in question. I have also realized that we broke our contract and for that, I must go. I have to leave, and although you were the most excellent student, I failed you as a leader. I hope you can find what you need in life as I am no longer able to provide it for you. Don't look for me as I will fade away in time as all memories do. My dearest Anita, know that I will always carry you in my heart.

Every day, for nine and a half months, I have read and re-read this letter. Each time was like a dagger to the hurt because it didn't hurt any less once I digested the words. The day Sterling came home like a wild animal, it seemed as if he was troubled and trying to escape from reality. When he grabbed me and took me up those stairs, at first, I was alarmed. But when I saw the desperation in his eyes, all I wanted to do was be his peace in any way that he needed me to be.

When he placed me on that bed, I almost hesitated because I knew that I had never been with a man before. I also knew that it was explicitly forbidden in our contract, so as a virgin, I thought I was safe. Until that time, it was one of those things that never came up because our contract said there would never be any penetration. So I felt no need to share that I was a virgin since sex was off the table. I guess you can say I lied by omission if we are going to get technical about it. But I was saving that one fact for if the dynamics of our relationship ever changed.

I couldn't dwell on it now because the man that I grew to love left me out here in the world. I was all alone with no direction, but there was always hope. I was preparing to leave out the door when I heard my phone ring. Like I have for the last almost year, I rushed over to it, hoping with all my might that it was Sterling. My heart longed for him to call and tell me that he had a change of heart. When I picked it up, I saw that it was just my best friend, Ta'iah. It was good to hear from her, but I wouldn't lie and say I wasn't slightly disappointed it wasn't Sterling.

"Hello, best friend. What warrants this call?" I answered as if she was the one that's been missing out of my life for months.

We had not been in contact as often as we used to, but she is still around, even if not physically.

"Sheesh, I can't just miss my best friend? Have I been that bad to you?"

Ta'iah's been so sensitive since she's been pregnant with the twins. Let me stop playing with her before she has a meltdown.

" Aww, babes, no. I was just teasing. Stop crying, crazy woman, and tell me how you and my beautiful nieces are doing?"

"They are fine. I can't wait to see their faces. I feel about as big as a house. I'm eating everything and not getting any exercise. I can't see my feet or ankles."

I started giggling because Ta'iah was always dramatic, and her antics were cute.

"You make it seem so hard. You are eating for three, so I'm sure your appetite has increased. Your journey to motherhood is a beautiful one. Just know that whatever you are facing is all to bring those new lives into the world.

You are very fortunate," I told her with a twinge of sadness.

I knew what she was feeling all too well. That feeling always led me back to thoughts of him, and it made my mood falter.

"Pooh, are you okay? Still no word on Sterling?"

"No, and I don't know why he can't face me. I forgive him, and I just want him to forgive himself. I don't blame him at all. I just hope he doesn't blame me for what I have done. He is so reclusive, he could be anywhere."

Ta'iah's question further irritated me, and I knew she heard it in my tone. It wasn't her fault, but I was frustrated. I was frustrated because Sterling never even tried to see if we could move past the breach of our contract. Per the letter he left, he made it seem as if we did something terrible and didn't share something sacred. I wished he would have just talked to me instead of disappearing.

"What did you do that would make him leave?" Ta'iah curiously asked me.

"I did nothing to make him leave, but I doubt he will be coming back."

I said that last part a little more harshly than I intended. I hoped Ta'iah understood that I wasn't mean. I just didn't even know how to explain the beginning of our end.

"Well, don't give up. You know I'm right where you are. I feel everything you're going through, but if you think that Sterling is worth it, wait for him."

"I hear you. I know it's not common to cross these emotional lines. I will cut my emotions off just to have Sterling direct me again," I said with more conviction than I felt in my heart.

It effectively changed the conversation from one of heaviness to our work which always made us happy. Ta'iah and I caught up on business and discussed our new product line. We also made a date to hang out, but I knew I wouldn't be able to hang out for a while. Honestly, I had been avoiding Ta'iah's presence like the plague, and for a good reason. After our little phone conversation, I began to feel a little tired. I start getting comfortable on the bed as I felt my body getting fatigued. I closed my eyes, contemplating a nap until I heard my door open.

My mom stood there with her body abuzz with excitement, and it is infectious. She came over to the bed and laid her hands on my belly. My mother's touch incites a riot, and the feeling made me giggle uncontrollably.

"You ready to go in and have this little rockhead boy?" My mom asked me.

"Oh, mommy, I've been ready. It's just my luck he would end up being two weeks overdue."

"Well, come on, sugar plum. Daddy already put your bag in the car, and we need to check-in for your C-section soon."

And there you have it. The night Sterling and I shared left me with more than memories. He left me with a permanent reminder of all that he was and all that we shared. It never crossed my mind to get rid of my son, not even when the loneliness consumed my soul. Nope, I vowed from the moment I knew that there was a watered seed in my womb that I was going to raise him and love him with the same intensity I loved its father.

I headed downstairs, and my parents are waiting for me. My dad helped me place my jacket on and then helped me down the steps outside and into the car. I climbed inside and got lost in my thoughts. I remembered running home after Sterling left. My mother and father never passed judgment on what transpired between us. They helped console my heart when I was inconsolable, and for that, I would always love them.

In order to deal with the pain of my broken contract, I threw myself into my work. I was barely eating and tried to do whatever I could to get Sterling's absence off of my mind. Many days, I only made it through by pretending that he was going to come home soon. One night, I went to sleep and woke up with a more than a noticeable pudge. It was hard to the touch, and I remembered screaming bloody murder, thinking that there was an abnormal growth in my body.

At my panicked scream, my mom rushed upstairs to see what was wrong. I asked her to take me to the hospital because I was a hypochondriac. With my weird symptoms, I had already written my death certificate. On our way to the hospital, I was checking google, and before I could get in and get to the back, I had convinced myself that I had a cancerous tumor.

Well, it most definitely *was not* that.

After a urinalysis and an ultrasound, I found out that I was five and a half months pregnant. The doctors were able to tell me that it was, indeed, a boy, and he was healthy. After that news, I literally laid in that bed in a state of shock. I was in that room trying to figure out how the hell it happened and I didn't notice. It was utterly amazing that I had a whole little person inside of me. Nothing or no one in this world gave me more joy than the little love housed in my womb.

We pulled up to the hospital, parked, and headed inside where we got checked in pretty easy. The irony was that being here felt like I'd come full circle. They put me in a room and helped me settle in before they come to place the IV in my arm. Afterward, they put a monitor on my stomach to help take my son's vitals. Soon after that, the doctor entered the room to explain the procedure once again, and it's risks, with me.

After signing forms and getting my blood drawn, the moment had finally arrived. The nurses came to wheel me back into the operating room. When we went inside, it took about twenty minutes to prep themselves, and me, for my c-section. I refused to be under general anesthesia because I wanted to be alert for the birth of the best part of me. We opted for twilight sleep where they would numb my lower region, so I didn't feel the incision or them shifting my insides during surgery.

The doctors allowed my parents to accompany me inside the operating room to support me through my life-changing event. My mother came to sit beside me.She was holding my hand, soothing me with her voice and energy. My mother's tender love and care kept me in a perpetual state of calm. My father stood at my bedside, looking militant as ever. It was as if he was standing vigilant over the procedure, and that helped me to feel safe and secure through such a major surgery. I expected nothing less from him because he had always been that way about his favorite girls.

Not even an hour later, a robust booming cry broke the air. The sound was more beautiful than a guitar lazily being strummed on a summer's day. My baby's sweet cries were sharp and bouncing off the acoustics in the sterile environment of the operating room. It was music to my ears. After cleaning my son up, they finally brought him into my line of sight. I couldn't hold him, but they allowed my mother to place him next to my face so that we could bond. When I looked into his precious face, I felt a love that resonated in a decibel I'd never known before.

His eyes were open and curiously surveying his surroundings. He was watching me as I watched him;that caused me to giggle and blow him kisses. My son's gaze made me feel like he was trying to figure me out. At the same time, I was trying to wrap my mind around the great blessing that laid beside me. I squinted, looking at his face and saw that, on his cheek, he had the same birthmark as his father. I could only shake my head because it would forever be a reminder of my greatest love and heartbreak.

But as I said, there was always hope. My hope came in the form of an eight-pound nine-ounce bundle of joy. I would do my damndest to be the best mother I could be to Baviyan Solitude Carter. I only wished his father could be here to share in my joy.

Chapter 15: Dr. Carter

I was sitting here on this plane with the love of my life, Blessed Holloway, enjoying the sights. Although this was a business trip, Blessed was an old school fool, and he demanded he came with me. He said something about how I wouldn't be out on a remote island acting hot in the ass because I saw some young muscled bound guys on the beach. That damn fool told me that Stella wouldn't be getting her groove back on his watch. I had to laugh because I loved the way he loved me.

As we were debarking the plane, I took in the beauty of all the things God, in His infinite wisdom, created. Nature was as close as one could get to understanding the perfection of the creator who created all creation. The sights humbled me, and I had to stop and whisper a prayer for the opportunity to stand amongst greatness. When we made it to the car, I saw Dominant and another gentleman standing there waiting on us.

"Hey, son, its good to see you once again," I said in greeting to Dominant as he wrapped me up in a loving embrace.

"Its good to see you as well, momma Carter. Let me introduce you to my friend, Zuri. He is here for support as well."

I hugged his friend, and his scent was pleasant to my senses. I might have taken a second longer than was socially appropriate because I heard my old man going off.

"Okay, lil' boy. Unass my lady, fo' I have to beat your ass on this beautiful island. Tara, don't make me bend you over my knee, since you're out here making goofy eyes at the young folk."

I smiled at the way he protected me. Reaching up, my hands tangled in his salt and pepper beard and pulled him down to my level.

"There will be plenty of time for knee bending, old man. You better be ready to give me all you promise, crazy fool."

Blessed kissed me passionately, and it had my lady parts percolating. What? I'm old, but this lioness still purred.

"You two love birds come on before I lose my lunch. Some things I don't want to ever to visualize."

Dominant made an exaggerating gagging noise as his friend Zuri laughed and went to grab our bags.

Blessed and I hopped in the back of the truck while the young folks packed our luggage away. Once our bags were secured, we headed on to our destination. It didn't take us long to reach the outside of my new client's estate. The estate did not have the grandeur of massive and ostentatious buildings. No, this estate was comprised of five or six cabanas' that surrounded a single level home. It appeared to be the only modern convivence around this portion of the island.

We pulled up in the front of the abode and proceed to get out. Dominant led the way as we entered the premises. When we got inside, I saw another gentleman and a lady. Telling from the birthmarks that graced both of their cheeks, I could only assume they were siblings. Dominant and Zuri went over to hug the gentleman and his sister. Blessed followed their lead before everyone moved around and took a seat. That left me with the floor open, so I didn't waste a moment.

"Hello, everyone. I am Dr. Carter, and I'm a family therapist. I have come to this beautiful island to assist you in your journey to healing. In these sessions, we will discuss some tough subjects that will test your limits. You will go through a plethora of emotions in this room. Just know that it must get worst before it can get better. This room will be a safe space for you, so know that what happens here, stays here. I was given a small overview of why I have been called to help, but I would like you to explain to me why you took this step." I said, addressing the young man that had yet to be formally introduced to me.

"That was quite the introduction. My name is Sterling, and this is my sister, Shelisa. I reached out to Dominant because I think I'm finally ready to *openly* deal with my past. I have been on a downward spiral, and very recently, it felt as if I had reached the bottom."

Sterling said that last part a little anxiously. I was here to alleviate fears, and I used my words to do just that.

"Well, son, relax. You have done the best thing you could do, and that was asking for help. I know that at this time, it doesn't feel like an easy feat. Trusting someone else to know of your darkest fears and nightmares take a lot of courage. Thank you for trusting everyone that's in this room to keep your secrets safe. I wanted you to tell us in your own words what you suffered through that led to you being on your downward spiral," I said to him.

Sterling took a deep breath, and I could see his sister grab his hand in a show of support. By his demeanor, you could tell Sterling needed all of the strength he could get to tell his story.

"It all happened between the ages of eight and thirteen. My uncle sexually abused me," he explained, then stopped.

"Okay. By uncle, do you mean a blood relation or family friend?"

"He was my mother's youngest brother, so blood relation."

"Do you remember the first time it happened? I know it may be hard to describe, but in the details, you will find your healing, so take your time."

"It didn't begin right away. I can remember I was about seven when my uncle was released from prison and moved into my mother's house. I was a very peculiar child. I still had imaginary friends and stayed in my room, preferring to get lost in fantasy instead of playing with other children. I used to see my uncle stand in my doorway and intensely observe me while I played. In my young mind, his being there didn't affect my imagination.

When I was seven, I overheard my uncle telling my mom that I was acting like a little faggot. He told her how little boys my age didn't have imaginary friends and walk around in pirate gear or with capes. He convinced her that I needed to be toughened up, or she would be dealing with a full-blown fairy soon. My mother took my capes and books and anything else I used to occupy my mind. If she heard me playing in the room by myself, she would come and whoop me. That is, until I eventually learned to stop playing by myself if I wanted to avoid her wrath.

Next thing I know, my uncle was taking me out to play sports when all I wanted to do was build robots and write stories. When I was acting like a *"little bitch,"* as he would say, I would be punched in the chest and berated. My mother never said a word against his abuse and turned a blind eye.

In my mother's mind, she thought that he was just toughening me up like most uncles. The hitting happened until I was eight. Then, he started making me come downstairs into the basement to watch "sports" with him. The first two times we watched a baseball game, but the third time, I will never forget. The third time started some of the most horrific times of my life.

On that day, when I went into the basement, my uncle had, what I know now to be porn, playing on the television. The movies depicted men who were being sexual with one another. The sight confused me because I couldn't understand how my uncle was watching the same thing he was trying to break my spirit for. I remembered sitting down but not paying attention to the screen as I sat with my hands folded, twiddling my thumbs. Then I felt him stroking my hair, which at the time was long. But my mom didn't always braid it so, on this day, it was just in a ponytail.

He started telling me how I was his special little bitch and how he'd been trying to make me tougher because he doesn't like bottoms, and he only likes to bend over tops. I had no clue what he was talking about when it came to tops and bottoms. So, I just sat there quietly while he had his hands in his pants, stroking himself as he stroked my hair. I could hear his breathing become rapid, and then he grunted.

After that encounter, my feelings were conflicted. Like, maybe it was weird, but I was a child that had no concept of sexuality. He sent me upstairs that night, telling me to come back the next night. I ran out of that basement, but that was just the first night of many."

"When did things start progressing?"

"To me, it felt like almost instantly. At first, he would just masturbate while I sat there quietly, but in a matter of weeks, my uncle started requiring me to touch him. The first time he made me touch him, I freaked out. My uncle had taken my young hands and put them down his pants. When I felt his penis, my heart started beating erratically, and I started screaming. In response, he hit me so hard that it knocked the fight right out of me.

That day he pulled his pants down and masturbated all over my face. His demoralization was the punishment for me trying to fight him. My uncle told me that I would learn to just go with what he said without argument. After I cleaned my face and got ready to leave, he told me that if I told anyone that he would kill me and bury my body. He reminded me that if I told that I would be responsible for the heartbreak of my mother and sister because I didn't follow directions.

Within a month or so, he started touching me in my private area. He would caress my young phallus while he masturbated, but after a while, that was no longer enough.

Then, he started teaching me how to jerk him off and eventually how to give him oral. The first time he ever orally violated me, I remembered throwing up all over him. All while I cried and cried and even bit him. He punched me in my head at that time. Then, made me continue while the vomit still covered his lower region. I remembered my throat feeling raw and crying, but that seemed just to fuel his gratification."

Sterling paused to take a break, and I allowed him to gather his thoughts. I viewed his sister and even his friends after he shared, and they all were a little misty-eyed. I knew this was going to be difficult for Sterling to relive and for them to hear. But this was a process that we had to endure. My prying would only get harder after this point.

"From what you described, it seems like you fought him and his directives wholeheartedly. Most abusers train their victims to submit either through force or manipulation. When was the moment you felt your uncle broke you into submission?"

"It started the year I turned eleven. Up until that point, he only had me watching him masturbate. Sometimes he used my mouth, or he had me lie across his lap so he could ejaculate on me and degrade me. That was until my mother told him that she suspected I had wet dreams. I overheard her asking his advice about what she should do to help me go through this phase. My mother's question gave me a sense of impending doom, but I didn't know how much further things could go.

My uncle asked her if I had started masturbating yet. She asked how she would know that I had begun. He told her me taking long showers, crusty socks, or books. She told him that she just noticed fluids on my underwear and sheets when she went to change them. He told her to send me to the basement when she left for work, and he would talk to me about it.

I cried that whole day knowing that I was going to have to spend time in that dungeon of secrets while it was dark. I hated the dark. It was the only time I knew I was unsafe. Well, that night before my mom left for work, she told me to be sure I went downstairs to see my uncle.

I pretended I didn't hear her and stayed upstairs in my room. Not even in those four walls of my room was I safe. My uncle came upstairs to get me, but he was acting differently. He wasn't acting harsh, nor upset like normal. He told me that he had a surprise for me. Like most children, I was more trusting of his niceties because we were naturally forgiving. I didn't know one child that heard surprise and didn't light up with excitement—happily forgetting the evils of the world.

So, with joyful delight, I rushed with him into the basement. When I got to the bottom of the step, I heard the lock click. Even in my excitement, I knew that noise equated to danger. But I was committed to getting a reward from him after all the creepy things he did to me.

Well, when I had time to look around, I saw that there were candles lit everywhere—soft music playing in the background. The scent of vanilla permeated the air and didn't bring me comfort like usual. I felt my uncle come up behind me as he began to rub my shoulders. I remembered flinching from his touch then getting nervous, waiting for him to hit me. He hated it when I showed an aversion to his touch.

By my shoulders, he guided me into the room where he handed me something to drink. I was so nervous from the anticipation of the surprise that I just gulped the drink down mindlessly. As he led me over to the bed, he started telling me how beautiful I was and how I didn't understand the feelings he had for me. He told me he thought I was ready to become his bitch fully and how he had been waiting for the time that I could fully enjoy his affections.

I remembered part way through that conversation how I began feeling a tingling sensation all over my body. My penis was getting hard for a little over a month, but I hadn't even touched myself before. In the basement with my uncle, my penis was so hard it was almost painful, so I grabbed it mindlessly, trying to alleviate the pressure. Then, my head started swimming, my vision became blurry, and I got a little dizzy.

He laughed a sinister laugh and helped lie me down on his bed. I started feeling like my mind wasn't my own, and I wasn't in control of my actions. As I tried to figure myself out, my uncle began touching me. Instead of the usual repulsion, it felt good. He started at my ankles and worked his way up, removing my clothing as he went along.

When I felt him grab my young penis, I shivered in pleasure. Very soon, he replaced his hand with his mouth, and I felt my body involuntarily chasing that feeling that it's warmth provided. My reactions were exciting to him because before I knew it, he was getting undressed and joining me on the bed. In my mind, I was protesting, but I could not connect my thoughts with my body.

He climbed up the bed and grabbed a tube of some type of lubricant off his nightstand. I watched him grease his penis up before he laid over the top of me. My uncle began kissing me, and I wasn't complying with nor denying his affections. I couldn't move, but in my mind, I was trying to fight, yet my limbs were not cooperating.

That nightmare started whispering how he was going to enjoy taking my virginity—telling me how no matter what happened after this, he would be sure to ruin me for all women. That's when he grabbed my legs and started pushing himself inside of me. I couldn't stop him; my limbs didn't work, but my tears flowed freely.

In and out, he went, telling me how good I felt and how this was the best pussy of his life. Inside, I was screaming because I knew this was wrong, and I did not consent. But still, he sought pleasure in my young body, and I felt my mind shutting down.

In my mind, I was in a faraway land where dragons existed. In that realm, I was a dragon tamer and had the fiercest dragon to defend me and my kingdom. Then, something I never imagined happened. My uncle grabbed my penis and began stroking it to the in-and-out rhythm he created. It felt like nothing I ever felt before, and I involuntarily moaned.

I had never touched myself, and this new feeling was more than my young mind could grasp. My uncle took that as my permission, so he sped up. I felt a tingling that started in my toes that rose into and out of my penis. I had my first orgasm at the hands of my abuser. My cumming had a domino effect because he came right inside of me.

Then, he laid down beside me, cuddling me as if I was his long lost lover. He told me that he knew I wanted him all along because my body enjoyed his lovemaking. He laid beside me, stroking my hair, planning a relationship I didn't agree too. I felt so small on the inside and confused regarding his thinking. At that moment, I finally believed everything he had ever said to me. It was like it finally clicked, and because my body betrayed me, I had no more fight in me...I am sorry, Dr. Carter, I need a moment."

Sterling stood up and left the room. Dominant and Zuri stood and went after him. I got up out of the chair to comfort his sister because she was visibly distraught. I didn't know how to explain to this family that the breakthrough was coming. But I was determined to mend this young man so that he could be free.

Chapter 16: Zuri

Could you say heartbroken? Now, Sterling has shared some things about his past with us, but he never described the intimate details. When he asked for a break, I knew he would need our support. Dominant and I jumped right up to follow him, and we found him out by the water. Sterling was sitting there with his knees in his chest, rocking back and forth. His posture denoted pain, and it hurt my heart to witness his breaking. When we reached Sterling, we both removed our shoes and sat right on either side of him.

For a moment, we all just sat there in silence as we listened to the waves crash against the shore. For moments on end, we were content just to enjoy the scene. As long as our brother could feel our support, that was all that I concerned myself with at that time.

"Do you guys think any different of me?" Sterling asked us in a small voice.

I knew he was wondering if we were judging him or questioning his manhood.

"No, you are still the same Sterling we have always known and loved," Dominant rushed right out and told him.

"You are still my brother, and no matter what you been through, it doesn't change anything. I just wish I could find your uncle and fuck him over real quick. Let him see what it's like to be scared shitless and become my prey. If I ever cross his path swear, I would kill him so you can have the peace you desire," I told Sterling with conviction.

I would give my life for the two men beside me. They are what, indeed, kept me grounded in this world.

"I really appreciate you guys coming here. I know it was hard for you to leave your ladies and my new goddaughters," Sterling said, trying to throw shots, but he had me fucked up.

"First off light skin, those precious little angels are *my* goddaughters. You know I will fight you about my little ones." I shut Sterling's shit right down.

"Whatever you little brown skin, bitch. I already called dibs, and they already love me more because I'm the best at anything I do. Ain't that right Dom?" he asked our best friend

"Don't put me in the middle of y'all gang warring. I already told you both that you guys share the responsibility. I have two children, so that means they have two godfathers," Dominant said, always trying to play peacemaker.

"Man, fuck that. I said what I said. Now get your, I need air having ass up so we can go in here and finish this session. It's almost time for me to be heading home to figure out why Zahra hasn't been answering my calls. She must like getting her ass spanked until it's raw."

"Aww, big bad Zuri having trouble keeping his subject in line?" Sterling asked me, and I looked at him like he was crazy.

"I'm having no trouble at all. My lady just loves the punishment. Where's your lady at again?" Sterling just looked at me with this faraway look in his eyes and walked past me.

"You about a dumbass. Why would you bring her up when you know she is off limits?" Dominant chewed me out for my slip of the tongue.

"It just came out. You know how we always joke around. I didn't mean anything by it."

"Get your block head ass in here and don't say shit else."

We headed back inside and found our seats. Once everyone was seated, I looked to Sterling and mouthed I'm sorry. To which he smiled and nodded his head and that was sufficient. I was glad that we were okay because my brothers meant the world to me. I never wanted us to be anything but on the same page.

"Now that we got a breather, I want to approach this issue from at a different angle. Is that okay with you Sterling?" Dr. Carter asked him.

"Yes, that is fine," Sterling responded

"Let me ask you about your life before your uncle came along. Sterling can you describe your early childhood?" she probed.

"It was a childhood. I enjoyed having a sibling, but my mom wasn't around a lot. I was the typical latchkey kid. Back in those days, you could sit at home by yourself because you knew not to answer the door or the phone. No one would guess that you were in there alone.

I remembered being happy and content, but in a lot of ways I missed my mother. She worked twelve-hour nights on the weekdays and sixteen-hour days on the weekend." Sterling told Dr. Carter.

"That explains a lot. So, do you believe that your mother had any idea of what happened or was happening to you."

"At, first I thought that she chose to ignore the problem. It was like she couldn't understand my non-verbal cues or my subtle cries out for help. She would refer to my not talking or talking softly as me being weird. Then, she would berate me for not being louder or choosing silence as faggot tendencies. Her unkind words made me stay in my room and pretty much stop interacting with my family. Honestly, I thought that she was blinded by her need to provide for my sister and me, but I know different now," Sterling told Dr, Carter dejectedly.

"Now we are getting somewhere. What happened to change your perception on what your mother knew or didn't know?"

"Well, when I turned fourteen, I found the strength to tell my guidance counselor. I had started hitting full puberty. As my muscles became more defined, my dick grew longer and fatter. My uncle for weeks had been trying to coax me to penetrate him. Every time he had me try, my penis would go flaccid. Afterward, he would beat my ass. He threatened to drug me again and make me sit on it like he should have done the first time.

I didn't know at the time that when he first penetrated me, he had slipped me a date-rape drug to make me compliant. To know that what I experienced was a heightened sense of sexual tension, due to him slipping me a drug to warp my senses, made me sick . I knew that I had found a way to endure all the vile things his soul created, but I didn't want to become what he was trying to make of me, so I told.

The day that my guidance counselor and the police came to support me as I told my mother about her sick brother, her reaction was totally opposite from what I could ever expect from a parent. Her words to me were, '*My brother, is not a faggot, you little piece of shit. I have no questions about his manhood, unlike your little soft as cotton balls ass. My brother is good to you and takes the time out to raise you when your father would not. I don't know if it's misplaced affections because he spends extra time with you. But if you fancy yourself in love or whatever it is that happens with your soft bitch ass feelings, then that's your problem. All I know is that you have decided to tell these elaborate tales because my brother does not feel the same, and that's sad. Just know that you will not get away with disrespecting my family name.*'

I never felt so low in my life knowing that my mom actually assumed that I was taking advantage of her grown-ass predator of a brother. That wasn't the end of her incorrigible behavior. My mother made me pack and leave that day, and signed over her rights before her brother was even charged. Then, when we went to trial, she sat on that stand and lied on me.

She told the jury that she saw me staring at her brother lustfully on many occasions. How she would catch me enticing him by wearing too tight clothing and always finding a way to touch him. The woman who birthed me even went so far as to say that I wrote stories about my fantasizing for him. She broke my heart that day, and I have never forgotten the moment she severed the ties of the womb. It was at my trial that I found out that my uncle was locked up for sexual corruption of a minor before."

At Sterling's words, I wanted to fuck his uncle up. He just didn't understand there are parents worse than his lying ass mother, and he was better without her.

"Okay, that's enough heaviness for today. Let's move to a lighter subject. With all that has transpired between you and your uncle, how do you identify as far as your sexual orientation?" Dr. Carter asked Sterling.

"I identify as heterosexual. I don't have feelings for or attraction to the same sex. Although, I had never really explored sex fully with the opposite sex, I always loved women. Well, I hadn't explored intercourse until recently," Sterling replied.

He whispered that last part, but I caught it. It made me sit up and listen a little closer.

"Do you care to elaborate?" Dr. Carter encouraged Sterling to continue.

"I don't know how to explain my point." That made me look at Sterling funny because he was a master with words.

"Hmmm, let me ask you a question. Are you a Dominant like Chocolate over there?" Dr. Carter asked him while referring to Dominant, and it made us all laugh.

"Yes, ma'am, I am a Dominant."

"Well, excuse my ignorance but how does your relationship work without sex? Why have you never had sex with your subjects?" Dr. Carter digs deeper into Sterling's life.

"Each Dominant requires something different. I use fantasy to make my real-life experiences enhanced. I have the same desire to control my environment and that of my Submissive, but I just take a more colorful approach. I use the mind as the vehicle that drives our world forward.

The reason why, is because of everything my uncle has ever said and done to me. It left me in a perpetual state of not knowing who I was to become. I was confused about my manhood and didn't trust myself to be with women when there was still uncertainty in my soul. I felt like I would wake up one day with a woman after building a beautiful life and upset it with possible dark hidden urges. I couldn't risk *it* or a woman's heart."

"So, you don't have sex at all? I mean, in any form?" Dr. Carter asks Sterling for clarification.

"I do have oral sex when the pressure gets too much or when the fantasies become very erotic. That's as far as I have been comfortable with."

"Has any of your Submissives ever desired more? I mean, you're young and handsome and walk like you are blessed in the lower region. I can't imagine any young woman in this day and age that wouldn't be trying to take you down to the ground." Dr. Carter said to Sterling, and a little breathlessly I might add.

I automatically looked at Papa Holloway because I knew he was about to grab his nuts.

"Tara Unique Carter, don't get embarrassed in front these youngins," he told her.

183

"I'm sorry, love. I was just making a point."

"Well, make another one and this session gon' be over. Stay on topic woman."

I loved how Papa Holloway laid down the law.

"You got it, sugar. Now, answer my question Sterling."

"There have been plenty of women who wanted to have sex with me, but once I knew that it was leading there, I would terminate the contracts. I'm a stickler for honoring my word. I also expect these women to be honest about their needs. So, once we sign the contract, we play by the rules until the terms are fulfilled," Sterling answered her inquiry.

"So, has there ever been anyone that has come close to perfection? Someone who played by all your rules?"

"Yes, and she was the greatest story ever written. I never met a woman more eager to please me. Who took my correction and applied it to life. My days and nights were complete because she met me at the mind. She was like poetry in motion. No matter how much I pushed, she accepted me as I was.

So many times, our time together would get intense and she never pushed for more. She remained content with the pace I set forth. Whatever I needed her to be, she became. It was the best thing that ever happened to me. For the first time in thirty-four years of living, there was no darkness because she was my safe space."

It was then I knew he was talking about Anita and their situation.

"She sounds perfect to me. What happened between you that caused you to end the contract? Or vice-versa?" Dr. Carter asked, and it was something we all really want to know.

"You see, about a year ago, I saw my uncle in the market. He approached me with the same mindset of a pedophile. It was like he couldn't see me as a grown ass man. I was just the little bitch he broke. For a minute, I froze because my mind started to replay everything he's ever done to me.

Then, I remembered who I was and whopped his ass all up and down the aisles of Fresh Grocer. But from his presence the damage was done. I felt doubt, fear, and like my world was slipping. I needed confirmation that I was no longer a victim and that my manhood was never in question. So, I raced home looking for the only comfort I had in this world.

There she stood brown skin, beautiful, and willing. I took her upstairs and ravished her like a maniac. I knew that salvation awaited me between her thighs, and I just wanted a feeling of home. With no preamble, I laid her down, and for the first time in my life, slid inside of a woman's womb.

But I found out that while I lost my virginity I took hers as well. The feeling was so complete, and she was so responsive and loving and attentive. After the first taste, I was hooked and for the rest of the night. I loved her and there was no feeling greater.

Inside of her I reconciled my past but knew that when daybreak came, I couldn't keep her. So, through the night I loved her with the deepest parts of my soul. But when the sun rose, I had to leave the only solace I'd ever known. I knew that I had broken the rules, *and* she withheld the knowledge of her virginity from me. The beauty of the moment could not take away that sense of duty I had to honor what we committed to in the contract."

Damn that was deep, and a little heavy but beautiful at the same time. I was happy he got that off of his chest. When I looked around the room, everyone was cool except for Dr. Carter and Sterling's sister. Both who wore the nastiest mugs I'd ever seen grace a woman's face.

"You know what I think? The bitch that birthed us dropped you several times on your head. We are no longer siblings," his sister said and left the room.

"Umm hmm, your 'bout a damn fool. I want you to go to your room and run that story by yourself a few times to see why you are the weakest link. Blessed, take me to my quarters before I'm tempted to find a switch and cut some ass all up and through here. I swear this generation is crack babies. He better be lucky he already paid me, or I'd leave his worrisome ass on this island to rot." Dr. Carter fussed while Papa Holloway escorted her out.

Sterling looked at us confused. He didn't understand what just happened because he was naïve to the ways of the womenfolk.

"Well, Sterling my man, that was your first taste of an almost extinct thing called girl power," Dominant started the breakdown, and I finished for him.

"Yup, it's a thing between women that can't be questioned, but all men can and will be put to trial over at some point in their life."

"Damn. I'm going to go sit by the water and think. You guys can do whatever you need to do."

We dapped it up and headed our separate ways. I reached over to my phone that had been on the charger for all of the hours we spent in the session. I was glad Sterling had a tower built over here because I needed to be plugged into the world at all times. I started my phone up and saw that I only had one missed notification. I hurriedly opened the message in hopes that it will be Zahra.

That woman was going to make me mess them chocolate cheeks up for her insolence. I wore a smile on my face thinking of the punishment she going to receive when I got back home. Zahra was always apologetic and took her punishments or tasks like a champ. When I opened the message and began reading, my smile quickly faded.

Chocolate Drop: Boy, you could never outsmart me nor keep anything I didn't allow you to have. Just like this pretty little chocolate bitch you swore was going to be yours to DOMINATE!!! Well, I had her first and she is mine once again. Don't call or Text her, and know that whatever contract you had with her is null and void. You can't have her, and don't even think about looking for her. Checkmate, bitch!!!

Immediately, I began packing my things and calling for my pilot. Although I wanted to be supportive to my best friend, I couldn't leave her with the despicable bastard that raised me. I couldn't allow Zahra to die like I watched my mother die. He is cruel, and he is sick. Every moment she was in his grasp was a moment I didn't want to play with her life. Now I had to go to war with my own father.

Chapter 17: Sterling

Four months of therapy on a beautiful island with a little lady that is no non-sense would have any man walking with a new step. In all those sessions, Dr. Carter helped me face my fears and find peace with my past. She had also shown me what I did wrong by ending my contract with Anita and never reaching out to her again. Dr. Carter cussed me from here to kingdom come. She threatened me to make it right or deal with her wrath. After a lot of thinking, I felt bad, but I wanted to focus on making sure that I was completely healed before I saw Anita again.

After what I shared about Anita, my sister stayed mad at me for three weeks. It made me remember how mean Shelisa was when we were young, but grown Lee-Lee could hold a grudge like no other. Once Shelisa got over her attitude, I was able to find out that my sister was also a victim of sexual abuse.

I found out that my uncle was also abusing her when he came home from prison again. At the time, she was thirteen, and when my mother caught him in the act, she decided to stop Shelisa before she could tell and send her baby brother back to prison. My mom shipped my sister down south with relatives with the excuse that she had been caught having sex with some neighborhood boys.

My mother could care less that the sick bastard took her virginity. My uncle had also gotten her pregnant, and she had her first child at fourteen. A child whom she had to sign the rights she held over to a relative.

Shelisa's story made me cry inside and out because she had to endure that fuckery. She told me that's why when she met her husband at eighteen, she didn't think twice about leaving and getting married. Solid was her light after so much darkness, and that's why she couldn't understand how I didn't see that Anita was that for me.

I was leaving the airport and had to take a moment to sniff the air. Almost coughed up a lung. After being around pure air and nature for more than a year, the smog and pollution of the city life was a drawback. But I could't lie, being back in the city felt good. I was here for one momentous occasion, and that was the Sip and See for my Goddaughters Dahmia and Dahiah. Zuri thought we shared the title of godfather but he was way off base.

I haven't seen the twins since Dominant and Ta'iah got married on my island. I was very excited and couldn't wait to see their little chocolate faces. I loved how they looked as if Dominant spit them right out, down to their little gray eyes.

I got inside of the Uber that was waiting for me at the terminal's exit. As I was headed over to their house, my thoughts drifted again to Anita. She was never really far from my thoughts. I dreamt of her and what our life could be. I often wondered how she would look full of my child. I had to shake those thoughts off. Everyone was not worthy of such a happy ending. But it did not keep me from hoping.

When we pulled up outside of their residence, I felt nervous as hell. I knew for a fact Anita would be in attendance as Ta'iah was her best friend. Although she never made it to the wedding because she was home taking care of a sick relative, I knew for a fact she wouldn't miss the Sip and See. Certain knowledge came because I may have asked Dominant a time or five. The inevitability of being in her presence made me shake a little. I didn't know how we would act towards one another outside of the constraints of a contract. It felt almost wrong, and I only hoped I could be normal.

Well, it was no time like the present to face one's fears. I signed in at the front desk, then again with security at the elevator. I liked how no matter if the dynamics changed in their relationship, Dominant still went above and beyond to make Ta'iah and his family safe. After getting the okay from security, I was allowed in the elevator. I took the ride up, and when the doors opened, it was like I stepped right into the motherland.

It was beautifully decorated, and the food smelled delicious. When I looked straight into the room, I saw my princesses in bassinets on a raised dais. They appeared angelic and laid out like they were being presented to the court. It was such a beatific scene. I headed right over to them to tickle their little bellies and feet and told them how much I loved them. After placing their gifts at their feet, like everyone else, I moved into the crowd.

I was scanning the crowd and it's many faces; I hoped I didn't appear too obvious. What I wouldn't give to look upon Anita's beauty once again. That was until I locked eyes with Dominant and we started heading in each other's direction.

"Look at you all domesticated and whatnot." I couldn't help but comment on how the married life looked on him.

I never thought that I would see my brother in a vanilla situation and be so happy. They always thought it would be me.

"Shut up, fool. How are you doing, man? I didn't think you were coming."

I knew he would say that, being as though I was underground for more than a year. My being a recluse always had people thinking the worst.

"I'm getting there. Thank you for referring me to Dr. Carter. You know I wouldn't miss the introduction to my nieces. *I am* their favorite uncle, you know."

I had to re-assure him

"You and Zuri are killing me with the competition. Since he couldn't be here, I guess you are in the lead."

We were joking back and forth. Our banter was interrupted by a loud squeal coming from the foyer area.

"Nita, oh my God! When did you have the time? Why didn't you tell me you had a baby? We could have enjoyed the journey together. Oh my God, he is adorable! Let me see him. Hey, little man. I'm your auntie. Oh, I love him already. Dominant, come look!" I head his wife express in jubilance.

Dominant and I headed over to the foyer to find out what had Ta'iah was so excited. When we got there, it was then that I noticed Anita. Anita stood there, holding a baby that appeared to be eight or nine months old. I stopped, and I felt all the life leaving my body. My mask automatically dropped into place. I knew in my soul that she couldn't have done the unthinkable. I snapped my fingers once and Anita's head jerked up. Good, she was still under my command. and any other time that would have pleased me.

In this moment, I needed to know if my eyes were deceiving me. I snapped twice, and she started walking over with the baby in her arms. When Anita was in front of me, she stood there with her gaze averted. There was no room for shyness at that moment.

"Eyes up, love." Anita looked at me with a watery gaze and eyes pleading for understanding. I would hear none of it. I wanted to see for myself what she had wrapped up in her arms. "Show me." Anita swiftly began to unwrap the baby. One look into his honey-colored eyes with my matching birthmark on his cheek, and I knew that he was, indeed, mine. I marveled at the look of innocence on his little face that mirrored mine. That face reminded me of the implications of her actions, and I was hurt and appalled. "Love, please tell me you didn't..."

Anita could do nothing but stand there and cry. Right now, her tears was not enough to justify the treachery of her actions. I moved toward Anita and I took my son right out of her arms. I then left out of the party.

As the elevator doors were closing I could hear Anita's gut-wrenching cries. Her wailing did nothing to stop me from leaving. A piece of me had been here the whole time, and I was completely in the dark. I could have been there for her. I would have loved to watch her swell with my young inside of her belly. She just didn't know how her secrecy made me feel.

When I arrived at the lobby, I took my phone out and called an Uber. Fortunately, it was not far away, and even more of a blessing was that my hotel was close as well. I hopped in the back with my son and I stared at him with infatuation while he watched me. I lifted him up to inhale his scent and familiarize my senses with his pure smell. He giggled at my actions then took his little chubby hands and grabbed my face. He blew a raspberry right on my birthmark, and that made me smile.

"Da-Da."

I paused, and he was just cracking up and talking baby talk. It caused me to cry. It was like he felt my energy and someway he knew that I belonged to him.

"That's right, lil' man. I am your father. I love you so much. I will protect you from the world."

That caused him to go into another fit of giggles. For those few minutes I rode, I just played with him in the back of the car until we got to the front of the hotel.

I got out of the car and rushed inside to check in. I retrieved the key for the penthouse suite and headed to the elevators. Once we made it inside of the suite, I went to the bedroom. When I was in the room, I laid down and placed my son on my chest. For a long moment, I let the fact that I was responsible for one half of his being soak into my awareness. I bounced him and threw him up in the air a few times while he enjoyed the time I spent doting on him affectionately.

After a while, I noticed him rubbing his little eyes. For the first time, I had the pleasure of rocking my heir to sleep. While he was drifting off to the dream realm, I began reciting a little poem that I made up on the spot.

Young king in the making,
You stand in my image,

The greatest gift to grace my lineage,

Love is found anew,

Life has a new meaning,

A new chapter is written,

I owe it all to you

I will raise you up solid,

Help you navigate this world,

No room for doubts,

You will have confidence within,

Just know with me by your side,

You will always win

No love greater than a father with his son,

You are the greatest parts of me,

Congratulations my heart you won

When he was fully sleep, I laid him down in the center of the bed. With amazement, I sat there and watched my son sleep. Watching how unburdened he looked, lying there, it made me think about how his mother did this alone without my assistance. How even though I wasn't around, she still bore roots to me—seeds, and helped him grow. I messed up the first time, and this time I would choose to do things different. I picked up my phone. I still had her number saved, so I shot her a text hoping that it was still working.

My Love: Meet me at the Marriot in the penthouse suite. I think it is time we mend our fences.

Now the only thing I could do was wait. I was finally ready to face my truths.

Chapter 18: Anita

I didn't know how long I laid in that foyer shrieking and screaming with all of the anguish my soul felt. All I knew was I never felt a pain with that much depth. How I got off of the floor to lying on the sofa, I didn't know. All I could hear was the soft mutterings of my best friend Ta'iah tellin me it would be okay while her husband escorted the guests out of their home. All of the things going on around me were inconsequential. What I wanted was the baby that lived in my womb for ten months. The child for whom I still bore the scar of love. One I wore proudly.

"Anita, you gotta pull yourself together," Ta'iah said to me, and I stared at her as if what she said, stunk.

"Best friend, how? Sterling took my baby. My baby is the only thing that I have that keeps me grounded. I can't deal with life only for it to keep ending in chaos."

A fresh batch of tears appeared on my face as I tried to appeal to her understanding.

"Why do you feel like your life keeps ending in chaos?"

I turned to the voice who asked me the question, and I saw an older black woman. I didn't know if I should answer her because she was a stranger. I turned to Ta'iah for help. She then turned to her husband Dominant who nodded his head in affirmation.

"Go head, Anita. It is safe to speak with her."

"I don't really know where to begin, ma'am," I honestly replied

"Let's start with the relationship between you and Sterling. Don't worry, I know that it is unconventional, so feel free to be as open and honest as you feel comfortable sharing. By the way, I am Dr. Carter."

Open up to her I did. I explained to her the beauty and perfection of everything we shared. I made her and those that were listening understand that our relationship surpassed the mental limitations of one's mind. It was like Kismet how our union correlated with all our hopes and dreams.

Then, I explained how he left and the void that couldn't be filled. How I survived his absence which really wasn't surviving at all because I'd been merely existing. Not an eye was dry in the house when I finished. It felt good to share my pain, and it didn't hurt so much anymore once I unburdened my soul.

Then, right before the good doctor could start helping me sort through my emotions, my phone pinged signaling I received a text message. Upon reading the message from Sterling, I jumped up, grabbed my things, and headed out of the door. I would explain my abrupt departure at a later date, but right now I need to be reunited with my son.

When I got to the parking garage, I hopped in the car and started driving. It felt like it was taking me years to get to a hotel that the GPS told me was only seven minutes away. I parked my car in the hotel's garage, jumped out, and headed to the trunk. Once there, I grabbed Baviyan's portable bassinet as well as the baby bag. Heading to the front doors, I hurriedly went inside. At the elevator, I was pressing the button repeatedly as if it would make the car come any faster.

When the doors finally opened, I felt like salvation had finally arrived. Hurriedly, I entered the elevator, then I pressed the button for the penthouse floor. The journey upwards did nothing to alleviate my nerves. I was bouncing from one foot to the other in anticipation of holding my baby again. The butterflies in my tummy were literally eating me up from the inside out. The elevator arrived on the penthouse floor, and the doors opened slowly. There stood Sterling, and his presence immediately calmed my anxiety.

Everything that I worried about before those doors opened, fell right off of my body like the release of a good exhale. Sterling stared at me intensely before he reached to grab the items I held out of my hands. Once my burdens were released from my hands, I took off running through the suite. The urge a mother had just to lay eyes on her young was moving all through me as I ran.

I found him lying in the middle of the king-sized bed; my son looked so peaceful. I pulled my shoes off and climbed up into the bed to ly next to him. I sniffed my baby like a creep remembering that his scent calmed all of my fears. I laid there transfixed on my baby's face as if nothing else in the world mattered.

"That is an amazing picture. Watching you with our son makes my soul stir. There has never been a greater moment before this one I'm witnessing."

Sterling told no lies, and I could only agree with him. When I digested his words, I did the only thing that I could think to do. I spread my arms out to him in an invitation to join his family in this scene. Swiftly, Sterling came to ly down behind me. He wrapped his arm around my waist and pulled us close. Perfection was what I felt as I settled into his arms and relished in our reunification. Residing in his harms felt as if he'd never left. This was comfort. This was peace. Although his arms were where I desired to be, I knew we had to address a few issues before we could move forward.

"I wanted to properly introduce you to our son Baviyan Solitude Carter. He was born through a cesarean section exactly ten months ago. I didn't find out that I was pregnant with him until I was almost six months along. I didn't really get to enjoy those moments that all mothers look forward to enjoying. But, from the moment I knew he was inside of me, I loved him fiercely.

I never questioned the gift you left in my womb. I was only happy that I would have a piece of you forever. Baviyan is a good baby who doesn't fuss a lot, he always smiles, and has slept through the night since I brought him home from the hospital. So please don't be mad at me for keeping him a secret because I didn't know he was inside of me at first. All I did was hope for the day that you would come back home and reunite with your family."

"I want to start off by saying thank you for him. I love his name and that you've kept my legacy, even in my absence. Anita, you're so strong, and I know it wasn't easy going through this all alone. It makes me love you for giving me such a precious gift.

Next, I want to apologize to you for leaving. There are things that you don't know about me that effected my decision making. I will allow you to ask me questions because I know that you have many. Over the last year or so, I've learned that in order for people to heal, they have to face their issues head-on.

I will be open and honest with you. All you have to do is ask the question. I want to rectify my mistakes as well as heal the hurt that my absence has caused your heart. I intend for us to be a family in every sense of the word. To do that, we need to lay all of our cards on the table," Sterling said to me.

I felt grateful and relieved because I had questions. There were so many holes in my heart, that I knew could only be patched from the answers he could provide me. With no preamble, I'd started my questioning.

"On the day that you came home and ravished me, was there something I did to make you act in that odd manner?"

"No, I had just confronted a dark spot from my past. My uncle who used to sexually abuse me approached me in the market that day. It made me feel like my whole world was crumbling. It was the hardest day of my life facing my childhood insecurities. I felt like that little boy getting preyed on all over again.

I subconsciously drove home with an overwhelming need to get to you. You had become my safe space and I felt exposed. I knew that if I could just be with you completely that I would no longer have questions about my sexuality. That day, between your heaven, I lost my virginity to you. I didn't realize until after the first time we made love, that I took your virginity as well. That caused me to feel regret because that was your gift and I took it from you."

When he said that last part, I squeezed his hand in reassurance because he had no reason to feel that hurt.

"Stop that because I have no regrets. You did take my virginity, and I am honored to have been comfort to you in your time of need. I thought what we shared was beautiful no matter how we got to that moment. What we experienced from nighttime until the morning was ethereal. That's why I was confused as to why I woke up that afternoon and you were gone. In your letter you blamed us both for you leaving. Was my decision to conceal my virginity really enough to end what we had?"

"I would say yes and no. If I'm honest, it provided me with a way out. I felt like shit in the morning knowing that I tainted something precious with my darkness. I would have never taken you so roughly. I would have made our first time precious. I couldn't look you in the eyes after the thought of my ruining you. I was ashamed of my actions.

I didn't want to stay and have you judge me. I didn't want you to see me while I felt so lost and uncertain. The next morning, the mind frame I was in, wouldn't allow me to be the leader you deserved. I want to apologize again for the insensitivity in my leaving; especially with just a note and no explanation."

It kind of hurt me to hear Sterling's explanation. I felt that, no matter what the circumstances were behind him and I joining souls through love making, it was still my most cherished memory. I appreciated his honesty, nonetheless, and felt we were on our way to mending our souls.

"Thank you for your honesty. I have missed you deeply. When you left, I felt so empty until I had Baviyan.

Our days and nights were perfect, and I really would like to continue that. I missed the order and the purpose our life provided me. I only have one last question. Do you want to sign a new contract?" I asked him and was waiting patiently for his answer.

"No, I do not wish to sign another contract with you."

When Sterling said no, it crushed my heart. My tears were threatening to fall, so I went to move out of his arms before I could start sobbing. Sterling pulled me back toward him, but I was fighting to be free of his arms. I was upset that I put myself out there, and he had the nerve to deny me.

"Be still!" As soon as he used that tone, my body went pliant. "Let me finish, love. I do not want to enter into the same contract we once had. I would like to do something a little more permanent. I would like to give you my last name, so that you share it with me and our son. I want to give you those same nights and days just with a twist.

Being away from you was even harder than I thought that it would be. In you, I have found my equal, and I want to enjoy this for all times. Do you want to spend forever being the manifestation of all my hopes and dreams?"

"Yes, I would like nothing better. I love you, honey."

"I love you even more, my love."

With that declaration, Sterling kissed me passionately. The lip-lock was so heated that urges I had not had in forever burned through me. Sterling got up to move our son over to the bassinet. When he made it back over to the bed, we quickly began undressing each other and reacquainting our senses with one another.

All too soon, Sterling was sliding into me. The way was made easy by my cumming before he was even inside of me. Sterling felt like all of the fantasies I had since he first touched me. He wrapped my legs around his waist and started digging into me deeper. I was ready to orgasm all over again as nirvana rapidly approached. I didn't hold back my surrender, and he soon chased mine with his own.

I could feel his life-force enter my womb, but he was not nearly done. Sterling remained rigid after letting go. He didn't even bother to pull out; he just kept going. And that is how you found us wrapped in each other's love for the remainder of the evening. We only stopped long enough for me to breastfeed Baviyan and to talk about our future. I was just happy to finally have my heart be whole once again. The possibilities were endless for our future.

Epilogue: Sterling

Life could have never been better for Anita and me. Our son was about eighteen months, and Anita would be making me a father once more in about three months. I was loving this new lease we had on life. We continued with our play time outside of our family moments. Anita was the light for my darkened soul. I was blessed to be able to absorb her sunshine.

"Honey, what are you up there doing? The car will be here soon!" Anita yelled at me from downstairs

"I'm coming, love! I had to grab my laptops and my passport!"

Hurriedly, I grabbed all of my items and made my way downstairs. Anita stood at the bottom of the landing looking ravishing. She stood with a hand on her belly with a smile that I knew was only for me. I put a little pep in my step to reach her in record time. At the bottom, I wasted no time kissing her lips before bending down to kiss her belly and talk to my daughter for a minute. As I promised my princess the moon and the stars, I felt a little set of hands on my back.

"Daddy, pick up," my little prince, Baviyan, said to me, and I obliged him.

"Bavi, my young prince, I am going to miss you. You promise to be good for mommy?" I asked my son who gave me a beaming smile before responding.

"Bavi always good."

I had to laugh at him because my son was going through his terrible twos early. I had to replace so many things around the house because of his curiosity. There was nothing like the shenanigans of a toddler.

I was throwing Baviyan up in the air and just enjoying this moment when we heard the doorbell ring. That signaled that it was about time for me to leave. We headed over to the door together, to greet our visitors. When I opened the door, I saw Dominant and Ta'iah standing there with the twins and their son in a car seat. We all exchanged hellos and goodbyes because Dominant and I had a flight to catch.

We hopped in the car service and headed to the airport. Zuri didn't tell us where we were going, but we would be meeting him and having the plans disclosed when we arrived on our flight. It took us around thirty minutes or so to arrive at the private airstrip. We got out of the car and headed over to the private jet with Zuri's company logo on its side. When we stepped inside, I saw that we had a few extra visitor's accompanying us on this trip.

"Hey, young men. We have to stop meeting like this."

I laughed as I walked over to Dr. Carter and kissed her cheek. Dominant did the same thing. I shook hands with Pop Holloway, and then we took our seats. We all sat there generally catching up on each other's lives They wanted to know about all of their grandbabies, and we happily showed them the latest pictures and videos. Both of us loved the new roles we had taken on in life.

We heard someone entering the plane. All of our heads popped up and landed on Zuri. My brother looked a damn mess. I hopped out of my seat and headed over in his direction. Zuri's eyes had dark circles underneath them, and his beard was basically touching his chest. I snatched him up in a manly hug, and he felt like he was clinging to me.

It hurt me that he had to go through this unnecessary trial. For the last year, we had been on a wild goose chase trying to find Zahra. Every time we would get close, his father eluded us again. The strain was taking its toll on my brother, and I wished I could take his pain away. I moved back from the embrace, and Dominant was right there to give him more love. After our moment, we went to sit down.

"We got you, and this time, I'm *sure* we are bringing her home. Your father has not moved from this location in two months. I think he is tired of running," I said to Zuri.

I had been using all of my resources in information technology to aide my brother in finding his lady.

"I doubt that he is tired of running. This was done deliberately as an affront to me. I have basically crippled his company. I knew that I would have stopped his finances, but my father is way too smart not to have off-shore accounts. But I know he doesn't have longer money than me because he was never a saver."

"Well, whatever the case may be, we are going to bring Zahra home," I tried to reassure Zuri.

"I wish I could believe that. It's just like my mother all over again. I only hope that I can get there in time and that my pride and arrogance doesn't cost me love once again."

"Well, why don't you share with us why you feel that way. The history between you and your father seems to run deeper than a mere family feud. Let us start at the beginning, and hopefully, with all this love and support, we will be able to come up with a plan that will ensure that we return Zahra home safely," Dr. Carter stated

On a long inhale, Zuri began to exhale his journey here. To say that no one would ever be the same after he finishes his tale was an understatement. After Zuri shared his truth, we are all going into this with a different agenda. Operation "Bring Zahra Home" was in full effect, and we didn't intend to lose.

The End

Zuri and Zahra's story coming soon!

All About Nadine Frye

Nadine Frye was born and raised in Philadelphia, PA. But coming from the inner-city never stopped her ability to dream big. Being raised in a large family, they all used our creative minds to have fun. Making plays, songs, and any other thing they could dream of. In her younger years, you could see her head inside of a book more often than experiencing the outdoors.

In her teen years, a personal tragedy unleashed a world of sadness and hurt only her notebook could understand. Songs and poems poured from her soul, and for years, it was to feel the relief from her heart. She began sharing small things with her close circle of friends. It was their motivation, and that of her mother and sisters, that she shares her talent with the world. It was the beginning of dreaming bigger.

She now resides in Washington, DC, where she wears many hats, including Mother and Wife, and she graciously adds the hat of an author to her line up.

Personal Quote

"Life is about evolving. Each day is a journey, each year is a teacher, and every lesson should be applied."

-Nadine Frye

Author Page:

https://www.facebook.com/PurpleLyricFandom/

Instagram: @authornadinefrye

Twitter: @AuthorNadine

Email: purplelyricfandom@gmail.com

Blog: https://authornadinereviewspor.blogspot.com/

CPSIA information can be obtained
at www.ICGtesting.com
Printed in the USA
LVHW091611061120
670968LV00002B/350

9 798653 102776